To Grace,

I hope you enjoy my second book!

Morgan's Series: Book 2

Morgan's New School

By KD Lee Writes

Published by Blooming Ink Publishing, LLC

4712 East State Road 46
Bloomington, IN 47401

FIRST EDITION

ISBN 978-1-943753-02-4

I dedicate this book to my mischievous brother, Darik.

Special Thanks To: DD, for being an awesome editor, to my mom, for being an amazing publisher, to my dad for helping me in many ways, to Gary for being so supportive, and last but not least, to Guy for giving me ideas involving the twins.

Table of Contents:

Chapter 1: The First Day of School

"MOM, DON'T WORRY! We will be fine," I said, hugging her.

"Well, good luck," said Mom. Ken and Sara, my brother and sister, who are twins, were going to school for the first time, as kindergarteners.

"Be good," Mom said, seriously to the twins. I had to choke back a laugh. When were the twins ever good?

"We will," they replied. They had been looking forward to this for a while. The bus pulled up, and we climbed up the steps to get on.

"Wow!" said Ken, looking at the huge bus. He sat in the front seat with Sara, but I went on closer to the back next to a girl about my age. She had dyed a strip of her hair blue in the front, and the rest of her hair was blond.

"Hi, I am Erica," said the girl.

"I am Morgan," I replied. I turned my head to gaze across the aisle. I was excited but nervous at the same time. What were the kids like? Would they like me? Were there bullies? Was the teacher a good one? Did they serve salads or just junk food in the cafeteria? All these questions whizzed through my brain.

When we arrived at Raccoon Elementary, my stomach flipped. Then butterflies appeared, fluttering around like mad in my belly. In spite of the irritating butterflies, I walked towards the twins. When I reached Ken and Sara's seat, they had already exited the bus! Mom had told them to wait for me on the bus until I could take them to their classroom! I felt my cheeks go red and hot with worry.

When I left the bus, I couldn't see them anywhere. This made me even more nervous than I already was! I decided to search the playground before the bell rang. I found the twins swinging on some low swings at the playground.

It was no use yelling at them, so I just held out my hands and said, "Come on." They hopped off, and I reminded them why they shouldn't run off like that. The bell rang as we entered the school, and I took them to room 5A.

"Hello there!" said a woman in the room. "My name is Mrs. Lave. What is yours?"

"I am Sara."

"I'm Ken."

"You sit right over here, Sara," directed the teacher, pointing to a chair. Sara sat down.

"Were do I sit?" asked Ken.

"You go in the class right across that hall with Mr. Lave. I don't have room in my class for you, and if I remember correctly that is where you were originally placed," replied the teacher, calmly.

"NO!" shouted Ken and sat on the floor next to Sara. "I am staying with Sara!" he exclaimed, while his face got steaming red.

"YEAH!" agreed Sara.

"Ken, please just go to the other room so I can get to my class on time," I said, pleading. *I can't be late for the first day of school!*

"No," he protested.

"I am sorry, but I have to get to class," I told the teacher and hugged both the twins.

"Morgan, you are staying... right?" asked Sara.

"No, I have to go," I replied.

"No!" Sara grabbed my leg, and Ken hurried over to grasp the other. "Get off," I demanded, shaking my legs. Finally, I just pried them off and ran out of their classroom to find my own.

When I reached the end of the hall, I found room 7B. Most of the kids had taken their seats. I found the desk with my name on it then sat down. On the desk were a math book and a paper that said:

Today's Schedule

(8:00-8:30) Math
(8:30-9:00) Writing, English
(9:00-9:30) Reading
(9:30-10:00) Geography
(10:00-10:30) Free Time
(10:30-11:00) Test or Pop Quiz
(11:00-11:30) Social Studies

(11:30-12:00) Lunch
(12:00-12:30) Recess
(12:30-1:00) Educational Movie
(1:00-1:30) History
(1:30-2:30) Science
(2:30-3:00) Study Time
(3:10) Bus boarding

I scanned the list of things to do for the day. Then I took off my backpack. I placed down pencils, notebooks, and other things I needed and put them in my desk accordingly.

When my eyes met the chalkboard, I saw written there:

Put your lunchbox on the cart and your backpack in the closet at the back of the room. Don't forget to take your things out. Return quickly to your seats. Remain quiet.
- Mr. Hopkins.

By the way that Mr. Hopkins wrote this on the board, I wondered if he was going to be strict. *Eek!*

I put away my backpack as I was instructed. When back at my desk, I pulled out a book I had brought from home to read. A boy tapped me on the shoulder, and I turned around.

"Here, pass this to the girl on your left," he said, as he

handed a tiny, folded note to me. It had "Valerie" written on it. I grabbed it and started to pass it to who, I presumed, was Valerie.

"There will be no note passing in this class!" Mr. Hopkins, our teacher, instructed, eyeing me as he walked into the room.

"I didn't write the…" I didn't get to finish the sentence before he cut me off.

"A class is for learning, not passing notes. If you don't want to learn, then I am wasting my time. I can't make you learn, if you don't want to. I can only strongly recommend it. Who wrote this note? Hmm? Who wrote it?"

"The boy behind me," I said embarrassed, hanging my head. I already didn't like my teacher at all!

"Come up here and read it to the class."

"Me?" I asked, sticking my book back inside my desk.

"Yes, get up here," he said. I did a half gasp/gag. I hadn't written the note, why did I have to read it? *This is so not fair!* I thought, exasperated.

I walked up to the front and eyed the faces in front of

me. I opened the note and read it in my head. It said: *Don't tell anyone, but I am going to move to Michigan soon. My dad got a new job.*

My head spun, he didn't want anyone to know except Valerie! Suddenly it hit me. I had learned a good trick from a movie that would work great right now.

"Eggs, milk, cheese, sausage, and bread," I blurted, the class giggled. I assumed none of them had watched the show that I had learned it from. It was unlikely they did, because it was an old TV series I watched with my dad. In the show, a boy, named Kevin, used the same technique.

"Now throw it in the trash," instructed Mr. Hopkins. I did and returned to my seat.

"Now that you are all settled and the interruptions are out of the way…" he glared at me then went on.

"I can introduce myself. I am Mr. Hopkins. Please bring out all your colored folders you were asked to buy." There was a rustle in the class till everyone had grabbed them out. Then the teacher spoke again, "You in the front row with the red shirt, would you please pass out a sheet of labels to each of your classmates, including me and yourself?"

When they were passed to me, I looked at them. They were blank, white rectangles on a sheet. When he was done our teacher said, "Please write your first name on one of them and stick it to your shirt." After the class was finished doing that, he held up a green folder.

"Stick a sticker on the top left corner of your green folder and write Science." When the class was ready, he did the same with a purple folder. "Put a sticker on the top left corner and write Math."

We were to write Writing on the orange sticker, Social Studies on the yellow sticker, History and Geography on the blue sticker, Reading on the red sticker, etc.

"Now we have time for a bit of math before we go on to writing," said Hopkins. He asked us to open our books to page five and begin. I only had time for five questions, when he said it was time for writing. I put away my math book, and he continued to speak.

"Now I want you all to write a full-page report about yourself. After you finish, I would like you to fix any mistakes before returning it to me in this box on my desk. If you don't finish in time, then you can finish in free time where you can catch up on other things as well. You have a half an hour. Begin!" Lead hit paper at that last word. I thought about what I should write, then slowly began my report.

My name is Morgan. I have lived in Indiana all my life. I like to swim, walk, bike ride, run, play in our treehouse and other things. I have a brother and a sister. They are twins. Sara and Ken are their names. They are five. This is their first time going to school. They have to be in separate classrooms.

I just moved to this town from a town that is two and a half hours away by car. My favorite restaurant is Avers. My favorite food is pizza. My favorite board game is Monopoly.

I am nine, but will be ten soon. My favorite subject is science. I really like to do experiments. My favorite animal is a dolphin. They are fun to watch. I like to watch them jump out of the ocean.

When we went on a vacation two years ago, we went to Florida, and when we were at the beach, two dolphins were doing tricks like summersaults, spins and other cool tricks. I also found some cool wild life like three crabs, a snail and many lizards!

- Morgan

I looked through it a few times then walked up to the teacher's desk and set it in the small box.

"You can read while you wait. There still are five minutes left," he said, and I nodded. Quickly, I grabbed my book and read a few pages. Soon the teacher interrupted the class with his annoying, raspy voice. "If you are finished please bring up your papers. If not, put it into your writing folder. I will tell you when you can finish it later today. Now we have reading. Usually I would let you have free read to read whatever you want, but I would like you to read this book on Indiana and have it finished by the end of the week. You will have a test on it; don't skip read. If you want, you can free read and read some of this book tonight at home; it is your choice."

He paused, looked at me and added, "Morgan, could you please come up here and take a book for each of the students?" I passed out a book to each one of my class members then settled down to read.

There were eighty pages in the book, so if I read twenty pages a day, I would have it done in four days. I read twenty pages, and then got out my other book. I noticed that many people around the room had done the same.

When I had finished a chapter in my book, the teacher said, "Now it is time for geography. Lucy, please pass out these books."

A girl with long, blond hair stood up, gathered the books, and slapped a book down on my desk as she passed down the row. It said: Geography Grade Five.

"Now turn to page five and do two pages. If you finish

them before time is up, go ahead and do some of tomorrow's work," said the teacher with his nose stuck in a military book.

I opened my book and saw the assignment was on maps. It didn't take me but fifteen minutes to do the two long pages. Since I still had time, I finished another chapter in my book. Then Mr. Hopkins looked up from his novel and turned to the class.

"Put away your books, and let's go on to free time. You may now work on anything you like. You can choose reading, math, geography, or writing."

I got out my book and read for the whole time. I heard the door open, so I looked up. Someone came in and took the lunch cart.

When I had finished three chapters, the teacher asked us to put away anything we had out. Then he said, "We are going to do a small test just to see what you know. It has math, geography, writing, spelling and a few other things on it."

He added, "Don't worry if you don't know it. You aren't expected to know all of this, so just skip the ones you can't do. When you are done just place it in this box. Tom, will you pass out the tests?"

"Sure," Tom answered and slowly slumped around the room. When mine finally arrived to my desk, I rushed to the first question; it was on math.

1. Caroline needs 3 1/2 cups of sugar for her first batch of brownies and 2 3/4 cups of sugar for a second batch. How much sugar does she need in all?

   Caroline needs 6 1/4 cups of sugar.

I used a spare note book to figure it out then wrote the answer down.

Caroline needs 6 1/4 cups of sugar.

There were five more similar questions, and then it went on to language arts, back to math, then to reading. It jumped from place to place. When I had finished all three pages, I felt like I had only missed a few. Fortunately, I didn't have to skip any. There were still a few minutes to spare after I was finished.

"Social studies are next. Max, if you would, will you pass out the books?"

"Yeah," he replied and soon was handing me a book.

"Read the passage and then answer the three questions. After that read in your book about Indiana, if you have any extra time."

When I was done with the questions, I only had time for a few pages in my book about Indiana. "Everyone line up, please, as I call your names. It is time for lunch. Don't worry, I don't believe in going by alphabetical order. I go by behavior and grades," Mr. Hopkins glared at me again.

"Since today I don't know who the best in class is, I will call people randomly."

Surprise, surprise. I was picked last. I could tell this would be a long, long year! I had never been on the teacher's bad side before. I thought I was a good student, getting A's and not talking in class. *Boy has that changed, and I wasn't even the one who wrote the note! So unfair!*

When everyone was in the line, the teacher said, "Ok, now please listen. If you brought your lunch, it will be on a cart when we get to the cafeteria. If you didn't bring your lunch, go to the hot lunch line. On Wednesdays and Fridays the school provides salad as well."

He opened the door to the hallway. We walked in a single file all the way to the cafeteria. No one talked; they were too worried that Hopkins would catch them at it. I got into the line when I reached it. I picked out french fries, mac & cheese, fruit cocktail, and a carton of milk.

After I had chosen my lunch, I sat down next to some kids a bit older than me. Then I noticed Erica and decided to move next to her. She seemed happy to see me.

Erica struck up a conversation as soon as I sat down, "Hey, Morgan! I don't know anyone here. Could you introduce me to a few people? My family and I just moved here from Iowa."

"I am new here, too! I just moved from out of town! I don't know anyone but you, so far," I said, beaming. I wasn't the only new kid!

"I have met you and one kid named Violet," said Erica.

Maybe I will have a friend by the end of the day. I hope so. She seems really nice.

"AHH!" screamed Erica, as she spit out part of her sandwich.

"What is it?!" I asked her, jerking with fright.

"Eric! My little brother put worms in my sandwich! I get so sick of his little pranks! Ugh! That tastes so disgusting!"

"I have a little brother and sister. They are fraternal twins and are always causing trouble. They're five."

"My brother is almost six."

"Which class is he in?" I asked.

"Mr. Lave, I think, since he is still five. He was put in the kindergarten class."

The loud speakers crackled and a booming voice announced, "Miss Sill, will you please report to the principal's office. Miss Taffer would you show Miss Sill the way?"

Erica grimaced, "I feel sorry for whoever is going to her office. She isn't nice at all! I heard from Violet that she is super strict, and sometimes she even yells at kids! Can you believe that?"

"I think she means me," I whimpered, quietly. "My last name is Sill."

"What did you do?!" Erica asked, wiping her tongue with a napkin, probably trying to get rid of the worm taste.

"I have no idea!" I said. Getting up slowly, I crept to the

cafeteria doors. I stood there pondering which way to go to get to the principal's office.

Chapter 2: The Principal's Office

A GIRL SKIPPED UP TO ME. "Hi! I am Elma Lawese Taffer!" she said, shaking my hand.

"I am Morgan," I said, wondering if I should have said my whole name like she did. We pushed on the cafeteria doors, and she frolicked ahead. I tailed her down the halls.

When I got to the principal's office, she knocked on a door. "Just wait here," said Elma, and she skipped merrily back to the cafeteria. I bet she was glad she wasn't me.

Man, I was worried! I had never been to the principal's office for bad behavior! *That must be it. Maybe I didn't do anything wrong. Maybe she is just welcoming me to the new school. That's got to be it!* I thought.

"Come in!" said a loud, stern, and clear voice. I slowly opened the door and took a seat by her desk, after shutting the door, properly. Then I made sure I had good posture and waited to hear why I was there.

"Your siblings have been causing a lot of trouble, and I was hoping you could straighten them up. They drew on the walls, they keep screaming, and they wanted to be in the same classroom together. We decided since they are siblings, we would make an exception and put them both in Mrs. Lave's class, but they still are causing a ruckus. The other students are having trouble concentrating! They keep asking for you too, so could you please help out?"

"Yeah, sure," I said, relived I wasn't in trouble! I should have known. Of course it was the twins! I followed the principal to their class. We found them tearing up some pictures that had once been on the wall.

"Sara! Ken! Stop it! This is a public place and you have to be on your best behavior!"

"But I don't like Mrs. Lave!" whined Sara.

"She tried to make us sing the alphabet with her!" said Ken.

"We aren't babies!" exclaimed Sara.

"Well, I bet you can't sing the Alphabet Song," I said, to trick them into singing it. I turned to Mrs. Lave. "Maybe they were just too embarrassed that they couldn't sing it," I suggested to her, shrugged my shoulders and winked.

"I think that must be it!" Mrs. Lave agreed, hopeful they would take the bait.

"But we CAN sing the Alphabet Song!" argued Sara and Ken.

"Well, if you could, you would be showing everybody how good you are at it."

At my words Sara and Ken sang loudly finishing it off with, "Next time won't you sing with me? See we can do it!" they exclaimed.

"Well, from now on, maybe you should show everybody how good you are at everything in the class! Even good behavior," I said.

"Ok!" they said, excitedly. I left with the principal just as I had come. Once we were way out of ear shot, she winked and whispered, "Good job."

She escorted me to the outdoor park since it was now recess. Then she told a nearby teacher, on watch, to ask the lunch lady if she would bring me some food.

The playground, itself, was tiny. There was a small slide,

exercising bars, and on the other side of the playground was a set of swings.

Beyond the playground there was a soccer field, baseball field, a basketball court, a large area with just grass, and a sidewalk around all of it, with trees boarding the left side.

It was fenced off except for a large tree with many vines and low sturdy branches. It was surrounded with rubber and foam to cushion you if you fell.

After I ate some of the meal the lunch lady had brought out for me, a boy walked up to me. "Hey, Morgan, right?" I nodded. It was the boy who had asked me to pass the note for him.

"I just wanted to thank you for not reading what my note actually said out loud. So thanks, dude; that was cool of you," he said.

"Oh, yeah, no problem," I said, in return.

"My name is Mark by the way." He bit his lip and ran off to the soccer field.

After that I decided to search for Erica. It was easy to locate her. She was up in the tree with all the vines.

"Morgan! Hey! What happened back there? You left me

hanging. See… 'Hanging'… get it!" she said, hanging by her legs on a tree branch fifteen feet high. "Was that a bad joke? Whenever my Dad hears me tell a bad joke, he tells me to keep my day job… school."

"It wasn't bad," I said, politely. I didn't think it was that bad of a joke, also, I didn't want to hurt her feelings.

"Now, seriously, what did you do?"

"Nothing, it was my brother and sister! They were misbehaving, like always."

"That is good... I guess. Get up here; you can see everything!"

"Ok," I said and scrambled up the tree to where Erica was sitting. We were on the highest branch you could get to, because beyond that, all the reachable branches had been cut off to keep kids from going too high.

"I can see everything: the school, the forest, the playground, and the swings!" Erica said, in awe. The clouds above were forming magnificent shapes like a dog with a short tail, a mushroom, a ship, and some weird, deformed monsters.

"Look at that cloud over there," Erica pointed. "It looks like my old hamster. He died a few months ago, before the move."

"I am sorry to hear that. Do you have any other pets?"

"Yes. I have a snake, a turtle, a horse, some fish, two cats, a dog that stays small, a guinea pig, two frogs, a toad, three hermit crabs, a horse… let's see… am I forgetting something? Oh yes, a donkey named Toot, a sheep, and a pig. My dad has some cows, goats, and some pigs that we take to show at fairs."

"You have, like, a dozen pets, and I don't even have one!"

"Actually I have two dozen. My grandparents owned a little petting zoo. They gave it to my parents. Now they have even more animals than I have. Our whole family is big on animals. In my old house we had a big basement where we kept all of my pets, except for the donkey, the horse, the sheep, and the pigs. They lived in a barn and a field. My room was in the basement, so I fed and watered them every morning. At our new house, the smaller animals like the dogs, frogs, and stuff are in my room, because I got the biggest bedroom to keep them all in!" Erica said, catching a breath.

"Could we go to your parents' petting zoo sometime?" I asked.

"Sure! You will love it there! We even have a saltwater touch tank!" After we discussed the petting zoo, we played truth or dare.

"Ok, truth or dare?"

"Truth," I replied.

"What is the worst thing your siblings have ever done?"

"I don't know." I thought hard; there were so many horrible things to choose from! Then I remembered, "The only time they made me cry is when they got into my room and stole all my savings, (over two hundred dollars). They burnt it in the fire, because I made them mad by taking a bite out of their chocolate bar that they stole from me in the first place! Ok, now you. Truth or dare?"

"Truth!"

"Ok, what is the worst thing anyone has ever done to you that hurt you?"

"Well, last year on my brother's fifth B-day, he got a sling shot. But the problem was he collected a bunch of rocks and sling-shot them at me. I got hit in the eye, and I got a black eye. You could tell it was there for over a week! I was lucky I didn't go blind! He also got me in the arm and the leg as I was running away."

"That is awful!" I cried, putting my hand to my face, gasping.

"So, truth or dare?"

"I think I am going to do a dare," I replied, hoping I wouldn't regret it.

"Go to the teacher and…" Erica paused for a moment. "Tell her that you saw a ghost!"

"Oh come on! I might get in trouble or something!"

"Well, if you don't do it, I win and the game is over, since we are the only two playing."

"Which teacher?" I asked, secretly crossing my toes it wouldn't be Mr. Hopkins.

"Mrs. Sledder. She is supposed to be the strictest teacher. She teaches gym Wednesday and Friday, and since it is a Monday, she just helps keep track of the kids at recces.

"Couldn't I just, like, walk across the top of the monkey bars or something? Please?"

"No, just do it."

"Fine!" I quickly climbed down the tree and jumped the rest of the three feet down. My knees buckled a bit, and then I slowly made my way to the teacher.

"Excuse me, Mrs. Sledder? I am under a dare, just so you know, but I am supposed to say I saw a ghost. So, I saw a ghost. Have a good rest of your day." Sledder just stared. She kept an eye on me all the way back to the tree. It gave me the creeps.

"Did you do it?" Erica asked, skeptically.

"Course I did it! Did you see her watch me all the way back here!"

"Ok, let's do something else now," Erica said.

"Like what?"

"We could go and play soccer with those boys."

"Ok." So, for the rest of the recess, we played soccer. Most of the kids didn't know what they were doing. There weren't even teams. We just kicked the ball around and tried to make a goal.

"Ok! Everyone hurry inside. It is time to watch a movie

on the disappearing water all around earth, and what we can do to save it," said one of the teachers.

Everyone returned to the school's doors. We rushed into the school, and all of the fifth graders were hustled into the theater room. Even kids from other classrooms, including Erica, came to watch it. We sat together for a movie on how pollution is hurting fish in the ocean and we are losing drinking water. Apparently only 1% of all the water in the entire world is drinkable. The rest is salt water. They also mentioned how to preserve the water.

Examples on how to save water were: to turn off your faucet while brushing your teeth, take short showers, and when taking baths, don't fill the tub all the way up.

When the movie was done, Erica and I parted to go to our separate classrooms. I wished I were in Erica's class. Any teacher would be better than Mr. Hopkins.

Chapter 3: Survived the First Day

FINALLY, when school was over, and the bell rang, I quickly rushed to Sara and Ken's class before they decided not to wait for me again.

I found them taking a toy phone from one of their classmates. I said, "Come on." They bounded over to me. We dashed down the hallway.

"Morgan! We were very good, and we were the only ones that knew the 50, Nifty States song!" Sara said, beaming.

We left the classroom, boarded our bus, and were off to the closest student's house. Luckily, we were only five stops away from home, because the twins were looking anxious to get off the bus.

"What is up with you two?" Morgan asked.

"Toby told us that at night little bugs come out called

fireflies, or lightning bugs, and their bums glow!"

"Have you never noticed them? They are out every night!"

"We didn't know what they were! We can't wait to catch them!" they both said.

"Well, they don't come out much until night, so don't think that you can start catching them right away."

"Ok," they said, sadly.

"When we get home, let's go swimming," I said. When the bus stopped at our driveway, we jumped out. I ran with them to the house. We all were hungry.

"Mom, where is Dad?" I asked, after we were inside and found our mom sitting on a chair reading.

"He is interviewing for a job," Mom said, plainly, as though she were very disappointed, but was trying not to show it.

"Why?! I thought you guys retired because of the fortune you inherited!"

"We had, but your father likes work, and he is hoping to get a job at Wells Fargo. It is good pay, but I don't get it.

He just told me this morning. He thinks we are going to use up all our money and not have enough to pay our bills. I think it is bogus. We inherited enough money to buy a few yachts!"

"Who is Wells Fargo, Mommy?" asked Sara.

"That is a place, not a person, Honey. People do business there."

"What kind of business?" Ken questioned.

"It's the kind of business where they take care of your financial stuff. It is the same place he used to work."

"And what does financial mean?" Sara asked.

"Ask your father when he gets home. Is anyone up for eating at O'Charley's?"

"Yeah," said the twins, in unison. I just agreed with them to make it easy on Mom.

"Get in the car then and let's go!" We hurried to the car. Suddenly the twins let out a whimper.

"What about the fireflies?!"

"We will be back before dark," I assured them.

***

Eventually, we arrived at the O'Charley's restaurant and sprang out of the car.

"Now behave you two," said Mom, sternly, as she pulled out her phone. "And be quiet while Mommy makes a phone call," Mom said, to the twins.

"WE WILL!" yelled the twins as loud as they could, just to be annoying. Mom put the phone to her ear and started to speak.

"Hey, we are at O'Charley's. Do you want to meet us here?" she paused.

"Ok… How did the interview go? ... Well good! So what do you think of the boss? … Good, see you when you get here. … Love you too. Bye," she said and hung up. "He will be here in ten minutes, so we will wait to order when he gets here."

"But I am hungry now!" wailed Ken.

"So am I!" howled Sara.

"Let's wait for Daddy, alright?"

"Fine!" said the twins, after murmuring to each other. We all went in and a lady with blond hair said in a sweet voice…

"Four?"

"No, we are meeting another, so five," The lady got two adult menus and then asked another question.

"Do you need two or three kids' menus?"

"Two," I answered since I wanted to order from the adult menu.

"None!" the twins exclaimed.

"No, you two have to eat from the kids' menu," Mom said.

"But we don't want to! We want to eat from the adult menu like Morgan," pouted Sara. Mom looked at me, pleadingly. She wanted me to order from the kids, too, so the twins would behave. I shook my head.

The lady quickly grabbed one more adult menu and a few kids' menus and said a little less cheerfully, "Right this way." We followed her to the table. The twins and Mom were still arguing when we sat down.

"We want to eat off the adult menu like Morgan!" Ken copied his sister.

"Yeah!" Sara approved.

"But you guys can't eat a whole meal from the adult section! You can't even finish one of the kids' meals!"

"Then why can Morgan get an adult meal?!" questioned the twins.

"I usually eat the whole thing, and if not, I don't mind leftovers. You hate them!"

"Then I won't eat!" said Sara, stubbornly.

"Neither will I!" exclaimed Ken, crossing his arms.

"I won't breathe till you give it to me either!" pouted Sara. Sara had gotten that from "Despicable Me," the movie.

"Three, two, one, zero, -1, -2, -3, -4, -5, go!" chanted the twins. And they held their breaths.

I started to count to see how long they could do it. Sara made it to 26 Mississippi and then gasped for air, but for once, Ken could do something Sara couldn't! I couldn't believe it! He didn't hold it for much longer though. He held it to 30 before he gasped for air.

When Dad arrived, everyone greeted him. Our server approached the table to take our orders.

"Hi, my name is Ashley; I will be your server today. What drinks would you like to start out with?"

"Chocolate milk!" demanded the twins.

"Coke, please," I said.

"I will have iced tea, please," requested Mom.

I'll just have water, with lemon," said Dad.

"I am on it! Be right back with your drinks," Ashley left, and Mom continued.

"What do you think we should name the new baby?" Mom asked, out of the blue.

"Jewel!" said Sara.

"Jack, Bill, Tom, Harry, Dan," chanted Ken.

"Girls names, not boy names!" I said, rolling my eyes.

"How about naming her something like Hope or Rachel?

Maybe something simple and pretty," said Dad.

"Rachel is nice, but I don't like the sound of Hope," Mom said. I could tell her thinking cap was turned to high.

"I like Rachel too," I said.

"I like the name, Rachel Lee Sill do you?" Mom asked, looking around at us for approval.

Everyone agreed it was the best name so far. That is when Ashley came back and handed us our drinks. "Are y'all ready to order, or do you need a few moments to consider?"

We hadn't even picked up our menus, so we quickly fumbled to open them. We looked them over, trying to decide what to choose. The twins, however, were ready.

"We will have the biggest burger on the 'A-D-U-L-T' menu," said Sara (spelling out "adult"). Ken leaned in and whispered, "Sara, how do you know if she can spell?" Sara nodded.

"Sorry, we will have the biggest burger on the *ADULT* menu, please," Sara smiled and tried to act adorable.

The waitress looked annoyed, and in her defense replied,

"I can spell, and frankly, I am surprised you can," she huffed.

Sara looked annoyed, too, at this point. I was surprised Mom and Dad weren't breaking it up, but they were probably amused.

"Why? Is it because you couldn't spell when you were our age?" mocked Ken. I stared at him with admiration for a second. That was a good comeback.

At this point, Mom and Dad pitched in. "Ok, that is enough. I am sorry…"

"Ashley, my name is Ashley."

"We are sorry, Ashley. The twins will have the chicken tenders from the children's menu. Morgan, what would you like?"

I decided on the petite steak and mashed potatoes.

Mom and Dad finished giving their orders, and the waitress turned around and stormed away.

When our food was served to us, we ate hungrily. Sara and Ken were so hungry; they didn't have time to complain that the chicken tenders were from the children's menu. When everyone was finished, Dad paid the bill, and the twins claimed they had to go to the restroom.

"Ok, Ken, you go in with your dad and Sara, you can go with Morgan and me."

I didn't complain even though I would never, in a million years; wish to voluntarily be in the same bathroom as Sara. But Mom looked tired and worn out, like after a terrible day at work. I wondered what was wrong, but instead of letting my curiosity get the best of me, I followed her to the bathroom that a cleaning lady had just departed. It was pretty clean. She seemed to have done a fairly good job.

Mom took Sara into one of the stalls. I waited outside looking in the mirror. I didn't do this often since I thought I was a bit ugly. When I was younger, people used to comment to me on how cute I was. People still say I am very pretty, but I don't agree with them. My hair is neither curly, nor straight. It is just wavy, and my eyes are too plain. Nothing is unique or different about me, and I look too pale. Maybe if I had a bit of color, I wouldn't look quite so bad. I thought baring my teeth to see if any food was wedged in-between my canines.

I heard the toilet flush and turned around. Sara came out with her hands spread out like she was trying not to touch anything. Mom lifted Sara to the sink so she could wash her hands. Next, Sara sat down on the floor, and she laid down flat. Yuck! Can you believe it? She stretched out right smack in the middle of the gross bathroom floor. Luckily, it had just been mopped.

"Sara! What are you doing! Get up, now!" Mom ordered and grabbed Sara by the hands, pulling her to her feet. Sara lifted up her feet and started swinging side to side

"WEE!" she cried. Mom held her like she was a baby to get her to stop, and Sara threw a hissy fit, crying, screaming, and clawing.

"Sara, what has gotten into you?!" asked Mom, squeezing her tighter. A lady walked into the bathroom, stared at Sara and scooted around us, disappearing into a stall. *We really can't bring the twins anywhere without them creating a scene!*

Mom left the bathroom, carrying Sara. There was Ken sitting on a bench waiting with Dad. When Ken saw Sara he started screaming too! Normally they, at least, had a reason to fuss! But this was just spontaneous!

"Ok, let's go home," sighed Dad, picking up Ken like Mom had done with Sara. We rushed out to the car. I squeezed in the middle between the twins' car seats, and then Mom and Dad buckled them in. The twins stopped and smiled a big, chilling smile. What had just happened?

What were they up to? Were they trying to get home faster just to catch fireflies?

***

When we got home the twins rushed inside. They raced to their rooms to grab their bug nets from the closets. Pulling them from the top shelf caused other toys to spill to the floor. The twins left the mess and dashed out of their rooms.

"We are going to catch some fireflies! They howled, racing outside.

I decided to go out and watch. Sure enough, there were the twins swiping at the air. "Morgan, could you please go get a container for us to put these in." Sara asked, sweetly.

"Fine," I hurried back indoors and discovered a little pop-up butterfly habitat. *Good enough.* Once I was back outside, the twins had already captured a lighting bug.

"Morgan, look, I caught one!" cried Ken, holding the net down to the ground so it wouldn't escape.

"How are we going to get the firefly in the container without it getting away?" Sara wondered out loud.

"I got it," I say. All I do is lift up the net and pluck the lightning bug out of the netting and then set it into the container, zipping the door shut behind it.

"Morgan, do you want to help us find fireflies?" I shrugged my shoulders. *Why not?*

Thirty minutes later, when we were finally finished, I counted the lightning bugs as best I could. There were maybe twelve in all, each blinking their little lights on and off.

"What should we do with them?" Sara asked, staring at the fascinating bugs in wonder.

"When I was little I always kept them in my room overnight as a nightlight then released them in the morning."

"Let's do that!" Ken agreed.

We went inside and showed Mom and Dad our prized lightning bugs.

"That is all you caught?" asked Dad. "I remember when we would catch a whole jar full of lightning bugs in an evening! There just isn't as many lightning bugs as there used to be."

How sad and ominous, I thought.

We brushed our teeth, and then I put the bugs in Sara's room. Ken slept in her room for the one night so he could watch them.

Chapter 4: The Big Bad Wolf and the Three Little Pigs

"AND HE HUFFED, and he puffed, and he blew the little pig's house in," I said, blowing air out of my mouth.

"It is just like our family!" cried Ken.

"Yeah, because Mom is the Big Bad Wolf, I am the second little pig because I was born second. Ken is the first little pig because he was born before me, and Morgan you are the third little pig!" exclaimed Sara.

"Who is Dad?" I asked.

"Dad is one of the people who deliver the sticks and hay and bricks to the pigs."

"Why is that?" Morgan asked.

"Because that is the only place he sort of fits in the story!" exclaimed Sara, as if it were one of the most obvious things in the world.

"Ok, we will have to stop the story there. We are almost home."

I've loved my new house since we got it. My favorite part was my huge room with my own bathroom. I loved the fact that there was a pool! It was a big, in-ground pool, with a little slide and a diving board. There was also a small pool house to keep stuff in.

There was a treehouse, too, in a huge tree, with a creek right beside it. It had a deck all the way around it and a slide to go down. Just to make things cooler it had a rope tied to a bucket, connected to a pulley, to send stuff up to and down from the treehouse.

Inside we had a bench, a desk, a wooden chair, a play kitchen, and a little wooden bed with a place for a mattress to fit inside, all with plenty of head room. We also had seventy-four acres of woods and a big field to explore.

Today was the second day of school. Sara, Ken, and I got to go to the library to pick out some books. They got the Three Little Pigs. Sara got one on Barbie's and one on fairies. Ken got one on Superman and Spiderman. I got Hatchet, and the first book of the Sisters Grim.

Ken and Sara were supposed to read two books a week since the books were so short. Their teacher told them if they couldn't read (which they can a bit), they were allowed to have books read to them.

I, on the other hand, have to read 500 minutes every month. Every 500 minutes you read, you get a scale put on the dragon in the library. Right now, since it doesn't have scales yet, it is only a head. It will be fun to watch it grow over time.

The driver let us off at our house, and we jogged inside. It smelled delicious in the house, like Mom was cooking something. We went into the kitchen and found Dad studying a slip of paper. Mom was busy taking something out of the oven.

As we came through the kitchen door, Mom asked, "Morgan, would you set the table, please?"

"Ok," I handed Sara's book to her and walked off to get the placemats and silverware. I placed them on the table then put a large plate carefully down atop each placemat.

"Ok, everyone sit down; it is very hot!" Mom placed a slice of bread on everybody's plate. Sara's and Ken's had only melted cheese on top, but Mom, Dad, and I had pesto, cheese, and tomato. I didn't mind the tomato, but I would rather have had just pesto and cheese on it.

Then Mom left the table again and came back with a pan of mashed potato cakes that had been cooked in oil and were now crusty around the edges. *I love potato cakes. They have been my favorite food since I was the twin's age.*

"And last, but not least," Mom announced, "We shall have a, drum roll, please…salad. She set a bowl full of salad in the middle of the table and served us all.

"I don't want salad!" Sara moaned in her most pitiful whining voice, sticking out her tongue.

"Too bad," said Mom, apparently growing very intolerant of Sara's constant grumbling.

"I won't eat it!" wailed Ken.

"Me neither!" Sara said again. Mom ignored them.

The twins ate their potatoes, nibbled at their bread, and sipped a bit of milk. They asked to be excused, and they sprinted to their rooms to put on their swimsuits.

When they were finished changing, my parents and I were done. We set our empty dishes into the dishwasher. I left to go to my room to put on my swimming suit. I met the rest of my family outside.

"Watch this Morgan!" cried the twins, and they both

dove off the side of the pool, close to the diving board.

"Why don't you dive off the diving board?" I asked, loudly, as I sat down on the pool's edge and stuck my feet into the water.

"Ok," said Sara. She stood on the board, holding Ken's hand. They jumped up and down on the board, but couldn't make themselves jump into the water. Finally, they gave up and stepped down off the board back onto the deck. They jumped off the side again.

"Here, I will show you how to do it!" I cried and stood up. My feet felt like they turned into icicles as soon as I left the warm water. It was so cold outside today!

I leaped onto the diving board and did a dive. It wasn't a very good one because I didn't keep my feet together as I entered the water. I didn't go straight in, so my back hit the water rather hard. But it was a dive, so I said, "SEE!" and then swam down to the shallow area of the pool to stand and watch the twins.

"Ok," said Ken. He went up without Sara and sat down on the board. His feet couldn't reach the water. He did a little push with his hands and slipped into the water as planned. Unfortunately, he didn't push far enough away from the diving board, and his back got scratched by the rough edge of the diving board.

He yelped just before he hit the water and then swam back up to the surface. Mom (who had been floating on a noodle nearby) hastily swam over to help.

Mom pulled him to the shallow end and (of course) made it a big deal. She turned him onto his belly, resting him on her knee and examined his back.

"Oh! You got a few scratches! We need to get some Neosporin on that, pronto!"

"But Mom, it isn't even bleeding! He will be fine!" I insisted.

"Well, Ken, what do you think? Do you want Neosporin on that?" Mom asked.

He thought for a bit. He loved attention, but on the other hand, he probably didn't want to have Neosporin smeared all over his backside. Plus, he most likely doubted that Mom would want Neosporin in the pool, so he figured he would have to go inside.

Finally, he answered, "No." Then, with a struggle, he swam out into the deeper area. He was not the best swimmer and neither was Sara.

"Alright, but when you get out of the pool, I am going to

put some salve on you," called Mom.

Then Mom got out of the pool and turned on the faucet supplying the water slide. Water spewed out of a hose and rushed down the slide, making it nice and slick to slide down. Ken and Sara happily went down it multiple times.

Sara even got up the courage to go down on her belly! Ken tried shortly after her. They were normally fearless, nothing they couldn't do, if they wanted to. But when it came to playing in the water, it was a whole different story. You would think that they would rather get a mouth full of water going down a water slide then a mouth full of mulch playing at the nearby park.

But you just can't figure those two out! Like when they went down the waterslide head first, they said each time they did it, that they needed to wipe off their faces. So they would get out of the pool to dry off their faces. But they had had their faces wet before they went down the slide! *It is hard to understand how a five-year-old's mind works!*

When we were finished swimming, I decided I better do the homework Hopkins had assigned the class. All I had to do was watch a video then answer questions, and, of course, read part of the State of Indiana book. After I had read only a few pages, Sara and Ken came skipping into my room (without knocking).

"Morgan, we are bored!" they said, complaining.

"Ok, how about you two go play pirate or go swing or something."

Our new home was so cool. Not only did it have a swimming pool and treehouse, but it had a pirate ship playset, too! The twins got that in the summer for their birthdays.

The playset had four swings attached to the back. The ship had a sail, a wheel, and even a canon. There was a ladder to get to the top deck and a plank sticking out the side.

There was, also, a soft pad under the plank, so we could safely land if we jumped off it. The middle of the ship was about five feet high. The ends of the ship were seven feet high, so it was easy to stand up in the belly of the ship. There was one set of steps up to the deck leading to the ship's wheel. There was a trap door in the middle of the ship's upper deck that you could open and go down below using a ladder.

Inside the belly of the ship, there was a desk at one side and a bench at the other. There were also many small, round windows on the sides of the ship.

"You could play Barbie. I am trying to read my school assignment," I said. I was hoping they would find something to do that didn't involve me.

"But Ken hates Barbie games!" argued Sara, crossing her arms.

"Then he can use action figures. Just leave me alone."

"Knock, knock," said Mom, as she knocked on the frame of my door. "It is almost your b-day, Morgan. Why don't we think of something to do for it? I already have a list of family members we can invite from Florida and Canada; now you can add friends you want to invite!"

"Ok," I said, as she set the list next to me.

"What kind of cake do you want? Do you want a vanilla cake or a chocolate one?"

"Vanilla," I answered, "I don't want candy on it like last year's, just icing."

"Ok, do you want me to make it or get it from the store?"

"I'd rather eat your homemade cakes over the store-bought kind," I answered. Mom beamed.

"Aw, thanks. Would you like to come to the store with me, or do you want to stay home and read?"

"Stay here. I need to finish my studies. Thanks, Mom, bye."

"Bye," Mom said, as she left to shop.

Later, the twins, who had been silent for a while, interrupted my studies. "We were really good and didn't disturb you. So, can we please play zombie hunter with you!?" asked Ken.

"Sure, but only for a little while, and I will pretend I am sick, so I can keep reading my book, alright?"

"Yes! Ok, PLAY! Hurry! Our base is at the treehouse; come on I will help you get there!"

I put my arms over their shoulders and pretended my leg was broken, and hopped on one foot. When we got there, I placed my book in the basket. Sara rushed ahead to climb up to the deck and pull up the basket and to be the look out. After she got the book safely into the treehouse, she came out and screamed to us.

"Hurry, Ken! Get that injured lady up here quick! There is a black-eyed zombie approaching!" Once they positioned me down on the bed, I asked them what a black-eyed zombie was. Ken left and made sure it didn't get in the treehouse. Sara dabbed an imaginary wet rag on my forehead and explained the different types of zombies to me.

"The yellow-eyed zombies are slow and stupid. The red-eyed zombies are fast and stupid. The black-eyed zombies are fast and smart. The pre-zombies are zombies that just turned. They crave brains, but they haven't quite forgotten their past lives." I had to admit I was impressed that they made up all those different types of zombies by themselves.

Sara stuck a "thermometer" in my mouth. She told me, "You have a temperature of 153 degrees Fahrenheit!" Sara gasped, "You are really sick!"

"Please, please let me stay! I know that I am a complete stranger to you, but you must let me stay! I am in no condition to fight off the zombies by myself!" I gulped.

"Yes, of course, but you will be eating our food. If you promise to gather food for all of us when you are better, then we will let you stay."

"Yes, of course, it is only fair that I do so!" I replied.

"Oh, we haven't been properly introduced, I am..." Sara

paused, thinking of a new name for herself and came up with… "Emma."

"That is a lovely name. My name is…. Erica, no, actually, let's pretend it is Allie."

"Well, what a pleasure it is to meet you, Allie!"

"Same to you! Thank you for saving me back there! If you hadn't, I would have been dinner for some hungry zombies or even worse, gotten away with a scratch or a bite and turned on the spot!"

"There are few humans left, so we enjoy helping the survivors," Sara responded, with a smile. I did a fake cough and started to read. About five minutes later, Sara brought me an empty plastic bowl.

"We made some soup; would you like some?" she asked.

"No, thank you, Emma. Ever since (cough) I came down with the flu, I haven't eaten but five crackers and a slice of cooked mouse."

"Alright, then, I hope you are well soon!" said Sara. She left the little house to join Ken on the deck, who I later found out was named (in the game) Jim.

I read and read till Sara came back to the treehouse with

Ken and screamed "WE ARE SURROUNDED BY THEM, AND WE ARE SUPER LOW ON AMMO!"

"I have a bit in my pocket, only five ammo shells."

"Alright, well, that will help," Sara said, taking them from me.

I couldn't believe what good manners Sara had been using while playing the game. I didn't even know she had them! *She is like a whole different person: Sara one and Sara two, or Nice Sara and Rude Sara, or Real Sara and Fake Sara.*

I watched as they pretended to get rid of all the zombies surrounding us. When they were done they told me it was all clear, and that I should get some sleep. I told them I would pretend to be asleep while I continued reading my book.

When they "awoke me," they told me to get up and take the watch, so they could get some rest. After a minute I screamed, "There is a pack of red-eyed zombies approaching!" Because I had said that out loud, the noise caused a pack of yellow-eyed zombies to follow right behind the red-eyed ones. I "woke up" the twins, and then we were quick to evacuate. We had run out of ammo. We retreated to the big house (our house) and stocked up, doing away with all the zombies on the way back.

We clambered up the slide and the twins took the next watch. Ten minutes later, we ended the game by releasing a cure that turned all the zombies into humans again and wiped the virus from planet earth.

It was a corny ending, how they found a vile submerged in the creek, and it just happened to contain the cure. It was, however, five-year-olds directing the game, so what could you expect?

Chapter 5: New Neighbors

AFTER THE ZOMBIE GAME, I went to my room to clean it a bit. After that I watched a half an hour of the movie," G-force," but I paused it when the doorbell rang.

I raced down the hallway and waited at the front door, calling for Mom. (Mom had told me I wasn't allowed to open the door without her close by).

"Coming! Coming!" she called out and was shortly standing by my side. I opened the door. A friendly voice greeted Mom and me.

"We are moving in next door, and we wanted to say hello."

Oh, good, we will have new neighbors! I thought.

"I am Mrs. Buik. This is my husband Mr. Buik, and this is our son, William," said Mrs. Buik, motioning to her son.

"But everyone calls me, Will," he added while shaking my hand. Will seemed nice, friendly, and not at all shy like most boys. He was cute with slick blond hair and green eyes. He looked much like his father. Except his father looked like his face was sunken in. Will had some qualities of his mother without the stretched-out face that made it look like she had had plastic surgery in the past, (and the doctor had made a mistake).

"Hi, I am Morgan," I said to Will.

"I am Victoria Sill. Welcome to the neighborhood!" said Mom, shaking the small family's hands.

"Which house are you moving into?" asked Mom, peeking outside.

"The one to the right of your house," replied Will.

I searched my mind, but I couldn't remember a house there. I stepped outside and looked around. Behind many trees was a tiny house that looked only a bit larger than a R.V. It must have just been delivered to the property.

"That house there?" asked Mom, pointing to the house.

"Yeah, and we also have a five-acre lot," said Will.

"Would you like to come inside?" Mom asked. Mrs. Buik shook her head, no.

"Thanks, but we still have a few things to move."

"Do you need help moving in? We, ourselves, have only been here a little while."

"Oh, that is very kind, but we are almost finished. Maybe we can get together, soon. It's so nice to meet you. Goodbye!" Mrs. Buik said.

The door slowly closed as we said bye, and then I peeked out the window to watch them walking back to their house. Mom turned to me.

"Do you want to rent a movie?"

"Sure, I guess," I said, as the twins came down hall.

"Movie!" they cried. Mom turned on the TV and flipped through Netflix, first.

"Ok, let's see, there is, 'Rio, 2'!" she read. We could watch that, and it is free on Netflix."

"No, we want one that costs money!" cried the twins.

"It does cost money," Mom said, *which isn't quite a lie, since Netflix is a few dollars a month.*

"Ok, let's watch it!"

Mom hit play and it started. She went to the kitchen to pop some corn. Mom gave us popcorn ten minutes into the movie, and we all enjoyed ourselves.

At the end of the movie, I noticed the twins had fallen asleep, leaning against each other on the couch. *Aw,* they are *so cute, when they are asleep!* We left them on the couch, and I went up to bed to read a chapter of the "Hatchet" book for school.

The next day was interesting. I found out that it had been "show and tell" day in Sara and Ken's class by getting called to the principal's office again. Of course, I had to get called to the office when it was almost the time to go home. I wasn't nervous this time; I figured it was probably the twins, once more. I was told that they had brought worms to school, and Ken had stuck one in a girl named Pamela's mouth.

She had freaked out and hit Ken in the stomach. Both Sara and Ken had jumped onto her and wrestled her till they were carted off to the principal's office. To make matters worse, they would not give up trying to escape the office. The principal needed my help once again!

I talked them out of trying to escape and sat with them, while the principal spoke to them about proper school behavior. She even threatened to call our Mom, but she didn't.

When it was time to go home, I grasped their hands and dragged them into the hall where the kids were pushing one another, trying to leave the school and load onto the buses.

I was almost to the door when someone tapped me on the shoulder. It was Erica. "Guess what! I am going to go on your bus from now on! My old bus driver has a new route! My brother will be riding it, too."

"Ok, where is he?"

"He is… I don't know. He said he was going to go tell his friend, Dan, something and would meet me on the bus. You can meet him then."

"Cool, well, this is my trouble-making brother and sister, Sara and Ken," I said. As soon as I had said that, they stuck their tongues out at me.

"Hi, I think you will like my brother, Eric and his friend, Dan. They are probably even more trouble-making than you two!"

I seriously doubt that.

"Oh! There he is!" Sara and Ken let go of my hands to talk to him. They stayed away from us, whispering to each other, till my stomach got queasy with the tell-tale butterflies that come when they are up to no good. I hurriedly sat down with Erica on the bus, and the plan-plotters passed us to take their seats.

"Do you want to come to my house some time?"

"Love to!" said Erica, excitedly. "May I come over today?!"

"Sure, but you have to call your mom, right?"

"Yeah, here you call your mom, first; do you have a phone?" asked Erica. I shook my head no, so she handed me hers.

"Hi, it is Morgan," I said into the receiver.

"Hi, Sweetie! What is wrong? Are you ok?!" she asked, fearfully.

"Nothing is wrong. I was wondering if my friend and her brother could come over for dinner."

"Of course, they can, as long as it is ok with her mother. I am at the store so I probably won't be there when you get home. See you soon, bye!"

"Bye," I hung up and handed Erica the phone.

"Ok, my turn," she said and dialed her mom's cell.

"Hi,"……. "Yes,"……. "Can Eric and I go to a friend's house?"………. "Ok, sounds great. Thanks! Bye!"…..and she hung up. "Ok, she said it is alright!"

"My mom would never let me go to a friend's house if she didn't know the parents!" I exclaimed.

"Yeah, my mom lets me do pretty much what I want, as long as I tell her," Erica explained, shrugging her shoulders as if it were no big deal.

"Ok, cool. What will we do first?"

"I guess that we could, like, play a game or something; what do you have at home?" asked Erica.

"We have a pool, a treehouse and a swing set."

"Awesome! All my parents get me are pets," Erica said, sadly. "You need to come see my pets."

"Oh, yeah, I totally forgot about that, I have to come see your parents' petting zoo sometime!"

Erica nodded, agreeing with me. "For sure!" she exclaimed.

***

When we got home, we stepped off the bus. I went to the door and tried to open it, while the twins and Eric went around back. I found that the door was locked, so I presumed Mom must still be at the store, and Dad was, of course, at work.

I stuck my hand into the bush by the front door and felt around for the tiny planting pot hidden there. I grabbed the key out of it. Then I jammed it into the keyhole, fiddled with it a short while till the door was unlocked then I opened the door.

"This is my house!" I grinned, putting my arms out with my palms facing the ceiling. I put away the key, before giving her the grand tour of our new home.

After tour she exclaimed, "This place is big!"

"It is 7,200 square feet!" I boasted. I plumped down on the TV room couch, hoping she wouldn't think I was bragging too much.

"We better go check on the children," said Erica, nervously.

"Oh, yeah! I hope they didn't burn down the forest!"

Erica giggled; so did I. It wouldn't be so funny, though, if that actually happened. We quickly went to the outside and started looking for them. They weren't in the ship or by the creek, but as soon as we started looking up to the treehouse, something hit my shoulder, something hard! It stung like a bee and made my shoulder ache; it was a rock! Sara had Eric's sling shot! It was aimed right at us.

I saw Ken pick up a rock, put it in the sling, aim and shoot, all within a split second. I started running to the nearest tree to cower behind it, calling for Erica to follow me.

Another rock came hurtling out of the sky and hit my neck. I yelled, "OWW!" Tears filled my eyes. That one hurt! Bad! I was now behind the tree, safe. I heard Erica scream, as one hit her ankle; it was slung by Eric. She dove behind the tree next to me.

"The sky is falling!" Eric shrieked, joyfully.

Chapter 6: Our Guests

"ARE YOU ALRIGHT?" I asked Erica, worried.

"Eric got my ankle, how about you?"

"My neck and shoulder were hit," I said and put my hand to my neck. When I pulled my hand down, I saw something red. *Blood!* I must have been scraped by the rock! I grabbed a tissue out of my pocket and held it firmly to my neck, so my white shirt wouldn't turn red. I felt the liquid come through the tissue in only a short while. I crunched it up in a ball, so it would soak up more.

"Zombies! Come out. I have a nice piece of raw steak!" cried Eric.

I yelled, "Sara, Ken, would you like to be hit by a rock?"

Erica added, "Or you, Eric?"

"You are the ones getting hit not us!" yelled Ken.

Rage pulsed through my veins, so I told Erica, "I am not going to stand for getting bullied by five year olds! Enough is enough!" I was finally going to do something about it!

I sprinted towards the slide and walked up it, getting hit once by Eric. Then, I grabbed Eric's sling shot and threw it as far as possible. It hit a tree and landed in the creek. Next, I smacked Sara and Ken on the arm, hard, even harder than I meant to.

They let out a holler and burst into tears, even though it was nothing compared to the rock incident! Still raging and furious, in my scary, yelling tone, I ordered them, "Go down the slide! Now!"

Surprisingly, they actually listened to me and did what I had instructed. Eric stood in shock, too scared to move. Erica must have come up the ladder, because she said the same thing to Eric as I had said to the twins.

We led them into the house and Erica asked, "What now?"

"I don't know. This is the first time I've ever done anything like that about their bad behavior," I admitted.

I was scared, and adrenaline was still pumping through my veins. I was sure that everyone in town could hear my heart thumping against the inside of my chest. Would Mom be mad about what I did?

Right at that moment, Mom opened the door and saw the two strangers, one with a limp, one crying, and her three children. I was still holding an arm of Sara and Ken while they cried. They still had faint red marks on their arms from my slap.

"Tell me what is going on here?!" Mom yelled, almost dropping one of her grocery bags. She set them down on the floor to listen to our stories.

"Sorry, Mrs. Sill," said Erica, before I could speak. She explained the whole thing.

"Well, Sara, Ken, what do you have to say?" They stayed silent.

"I said, what do you say to our guests and Morgan?" Once again, they stayed silent, except for the sniffles, as an aftershock from the crying.

"Ok, well, if you aren't going to say sorry, then go up to your rooms!" Mom said, fiercely. After more consideration, however, she added, "But that wouldn't be fair for your guest, so instead, you can play with him now, but go to bed early.

"Yay!" they said and raced down the hall.

"I am sorry, Erica, that Sara and Ken did that."

"Well it was Eric's idea I am sure, and he has done it before, so don't apologize, Mrs. Sill."

"Well, aren't you polite!" exclaimed Mrs. Sill and then, changing the subject, asked us, "What do you both like to eat? I can make fish sticks, three cheese tortellini, spaghetti, pesto bread with cheese and tomato, or corn beef wraps stuffed with spinach and cream cheese."

Erica wasn't sure what some of those things were but, she knew spaghetti. "Spaghetti is fine, but my brother will want his with butter only. Oh, and if you are making meat sauce with it, I would love that on mine!" said Erica.

"Spaghetti is fine with me," I agreed.

"Alright, spaghetti it is!" said Mom, and she began cooking. Erica and I rushed up to my bedroom.

"Now that, that awkward moment is through, let's find something to do!" suggested Erica. She then noticed that what she had said had rhymed, "That rhymed didn't it?" We giggled and then searched for a game.

"How about, we play two-person Euchre!" I suggested.

"You will have to teach me, because I don't know how."

"I don't either, so let's play Crazy Eights," I proposed.

"Alright," she answered. So I grabbed a deck of cards out of my crammed closet.

"Do you want to deal or may I," I asked, as I removed the joker cards from the deck.

"You can, that is fine," Erica said.

I shuffled the cards and had Erica split the deck. Then I dealt eight cards to each of us.

I picked up my hand. There was a king of clubs, a 2 of hearts, an 8 of diamonds, a 5 of hearts, a 9 of hearts, a jack of hearts, a jack of diamonds and a queen of hearts.

"Are we playing it the harder version, where a 2 means you pick up two cards, a jack means we skip you, and a 7 means to reverse?" I asked.

"Sure, but since there are only two players, let's not count the 7's as reverse," suggested Erica.

"That makes sense. Your turn, the person left of dealer always goes, first," I said.

"Ok." Erica played a 6 of spades on top of a 7 of spades.

At the end of the round I won. "Good game," I said in a fake English accent, shaking her hand.

"Good game indeed," she replied, mimicking my accent. We burst into giggles, again.

"What now?" I asked, flipping through the deck of cards.

"We could go outside and swing."

"Sure, I haven't used the swings much since we got them."

"Well, let's go then!" said Erica, racing to the door of the bedroom; we scrambled through it. Sara was in the hall with Eric and Ken. Sara was dressed as a princess, Ken had on a goblin costume, and Eric was a knight.

"Help, help!" cried the princess, as the goblin dragged her off. The knight just stood there. Sara said to pause the game. (Pause game means everyone has to freeze, so the person can go the bathroom, and other things. Unpause is what they say when the game is ready to start again.)

Sara got out of Ken's grasp while he was frozen and walked over to Eric. "You're supposed to save me! Uh! This is your line. 'I will save you, beautiful princess!' alright, got it?" Sara didn't wait for an answer. She got back into Kens arms.

"This is like a play!" whispered Erica to me, and we sat in front of the door to watch.

"I will save you princess!" said Eric.

"NO, NO, NO! You have it all wrong! You are supposed to say, 'I will save you, 'beautiful' princess!" demanded Sara.

"I will save you, beautiful!"

I could tell Sara was going to burst. This kid was five, and he couldn't remember one line!

"You forgot the word princess!" Sara began to sob. Ken let go of her, and she sank to the floor.

"I will save you, beautiful princess!" said Erica and began to stand up to go the slides.

"HHAAWW! You are perfect! You can be the girl knight! Sadly, we don't have a knight costume that would fit. But I guess it will have to do," cried Sara, excitedly.

"Erica is going outside with me," I said, saving Erica from having to say no.

"Yep, sorry guys," said Erica and started to walk away with me.

"Please!" Sara begged, rushing up to her.

"Sorry, but I am going to hang out with your big sister, Morgan, for a bit."

"Please, please, please!" pleaded Sara, clasping her hands and using her cute little doggy face.

"Sara, stop it, ok? Erica told you no."

"Then can I come with you?" she asked.

"No, just play with Eric and Ken," I said. Sara turned around and started muttering to Eric and Ken, quietly.

"Let's get out of here. Something's up with them," I warned, grabbing Erica's hand and dragging her behind me. Once we were safely outside and on the swings, I began to speak again.

"Sara has a plan. I can tell. The way she didn't get mad and then whispering to Eric and Ken! She is going to do something, so watch your back."

"Like, what would she do? What do you think it is? Something painful like the rocks and the sling shot?"

"I don't know, but…wait, how did Eric get a sling shot? Did he bring it to school?"

"Yes, but go on."

"Well, it isn't going to be something we enjoy. I know that for a fact." I squinted up my face, deep in thought.

"Truth or dare?!" I asked and pointed at Erica.

"Dare!" she, cried.

"Hmm," I said thinking to myself. *Jump from the high end of the pirate ship? Too dangerous! Tell Mom she doesn't want to leave ever? No, that doesn't work. Give yourself a paper cut? Way too mean.* "Hmm," I said again. *Put mud on your face football style and act like you are playing football? Yes! That works.*

"Put mud from the creek on your cheeks football style and pretend to be a football player!" I instructed Erica.

"Ok, but, where is the creek?" asked Erica. She jumped out of the swing, landing on her feet only to collapse to her knees. She got back up, and I told her where it was. Erica raced to the creek. She sprinted back, pretending to have a football in her arm. She tore across the yard, and when she passed me, she threw down the "ball" and yelled:

"Touch down!"

I roared with laughter. I couldn't hold on to the chains of the swing, I was laughing so hard. I fell to the grass and rolled around, chuckling. Erica started giggling, too. When we were finished with our laughing fit, we got back on the swings.

"Let's do something else besides this," said Erica.

"Like what?" I asked. As if to answer my question, Mom stuck her head out the door and yelled, "Supper is ready! Come and get it!" She closed the door, returning to the kitchen.

Erica licked her lips, "Let's eat!" We raced each other to the house. I flung open the door. As soon as I sat down, Mom placed a steaming plate of spaghetti and meat sauce in front of me. Looking at our dirty hands, Mom requested we wash up first. Once cleaned up, we all sat down at the table again. Erica sat down next to me. Mom put another plate piled high with spaghetti in front of her. I dug in, eating hungrily, Erica followed my lead.

"Sara, Ken, Erica! I mean Eric! Come on! Lunch is ready! It is getting cold." A mini stampede of children came down the hall. They all sat down, and the twins began stuffing themselves. Eric, on the other hand, cut off a big blob of butter and dropped it into his bowl. He mixed it around and began doing the same action as the twins.

"Yum!" he cried.

"Yes, complements to the chief!" exclaimed Erica.

"I agree," I said.

"Well thanks, everyone," said Mom. She smiled from ear to ear and came to the table with her own full plate. The twins finished before anyone else, then started rushing, Eric. "Hurry up, Eric!" they cried.

"Sara, Ken, let Eric eat at his own pace." Mom barked.

"Eric, we are running out of time!" warned Ken, grabbing Eric's free hand and pulling.

"Just one more bite!" promised Eric, getting a big bite on his fork then scarfing it down.

"Ok! Ready!" Eric said. Sara whispered something to him, and he stopped.

"I would never tell them!" he insisted.

"Shh!" Ken said, peaking over at Erica and me. Then they raced down the hall.

"They are definitely up to something," I muttered to Erica. She nodded in agreement. When we were finished, we went down the hall to the door of my room. I turned the handle, but it was locked! I couldn't believe it! I had locked myself out!

"It is locked!" I told Erica, and she gasped.

"How do you get back in?" she asked.

"I will have to get the key, wait a sec," I said. I dashed down the hall and grabbed it from the supply closet.

"Here it is!" I said. I stuck the key into the lock and turned it and stepped inside my room. "AHHHHH!" a scream escaped me.

Chapter 7: The Trap!

I TRIPPED OVER A STRING strung across my doorway and fell face first into a bunch of mouse traps and the sticky bug pads that trap bugs. Erica stumbled down on top of me. Then some cold, liquid rained down on us. They poured water on us!

"Sara! Ken!" I yelled at the same time Erica yelled "Eric!" The twins and Eric were now sitting on top of us. Erica was struggling to get up. I was squished. I felt like I could barely breathe! I gasped for air and started freaking out.

"Get off! Get off!" I yelled at the top of my lungs. Erica couldn't get up, and I didn't hear Mom coming down the hall. *Why is Mom not running to help me? Why don't I hear her coming down the hall?* I screamed for Mom. I did not have time to feel like a baby… I seriously couldn't breathe! *I am going to die!* I thought. "I can't breathe!" I screeched.

The mousetraps under me dug into my ribs and gut. *It is not comfy to lie on top of mousetraps while four people are on top of you.*

Erica, meanwhile, struggled above me. Erica was skimpy and had no muscles, so no wonder she couldn't get herself up.

"Mom!" I yelled again, still no reply, nor the sound of footsteps. I felt like crying! Ken had slipped down and was now sitting on my head, so my neck was killing me.

"Guys get off!" I heard the door in the kitchen slam; I yelled for Mom, again. This time she heard me. She must have been outside before.

She pulled the twins and Eric off, and Erica rolled off me. I gasped for air, so relieved to be alive! Anger rushed through me, but I didn't let it escape.

"Are you girls, ok?" Mom questioned us.

"Yes, I am fine, Mrs. Sill. Morgan on the other hand…" she paused, looking over at me.

"I am fine, too. I wasn't at the time, but I am now," my cheeks burned with embarrassment. I might have exaggerated a bit.

"Sara, Ken! I know you have a guest, but this is the second bad thing you have done today! Go to your rooms and stay there till I come get you," demanded Mom. The twins complained only a bit, but soon they did as Mom commanded and were on their way to their rooms. Erica and I stayed in my room. First, we wiped the water off the hardwood floor then started trying to get the sticky traps off of us. Eric sat and watched. The traps were firmly stuck. They wouldn't let go of our skin! To make matters worse, we each had one in our hair.

We yanked and tugged, and finally all of them came off except for the ones in our hair.

"I think we will have to cut our hair," said Erica, examining the sticky trap in her hair.

"Cut our hair! No way! My hair is too short already!"

"We aren't getting these out any other way!" said Erica. "Besides, I am great at cutting hair! That is what my mom did for a living; before the petting zoo. She taught me everything she knew."

"I don't think I should let you," I said, worried she would mess up.

"It's no problem. Just help me find the hair cutters, a towel, a bowl of water or a spray bottle, and a comb," she said. I dashed to the "everything drawer," and grabbed the scissors and comb. Then I snatched a clean spray bottle from the garage and a bath towel from the bathroom. I walked back to my room and handed the supplies to her.

"Awesome! You found a spray bottle," she cried, while she gently shoved me into my rolling chair and put the towel around my neck.

"Now before I start, what style do you want? Like a plain short hair cut or have it be long on one side and short on the other? What do you think?"

"Just plain short hair sound fine, but be careful!" I said. Right before the scissors started snipping, I said, "Wait!" She stopped mid snip.

"What?" she asked.

"Cut your hair first, so I can see if I like how you cut hair." I said.

"I am not good at cutting my own hair, but I am good at cutting other people's hair. I cut Eric's hair, my mom's, my aunt's, my uncle's and their daughter's hair."

"Oh, alright," I said, unconvinced. She snipped the bug trap off and threw it into the trash can and began spraying my hair with water. Funny, how that is the only part of me the twins didn't drench in water.

She took the comb and ran it through my hair a few times. Next, she followed the comb along some strands of my hair and cut them at the ends. It was sort of weird having someone besides my mom cut my hair.

I had only gone to a beauty parlor once to have my hair cut, and, now, Erica was cutting it even more skillfully than my mom cut it. She snipped and combed and snipped and combed. It seemed to go on forever. I got more nervous with every cut. Finally, she spun me around so I could look at myself in the mirror and…voila!!!

I couldn't believe it…

Oh my gosh…

I blink again…

Not believing my eyes…

It was …

awesome!

She had done a great job! It was perfectly styled! I had no words to describe how I felt about it!

"Thanks, Erica! It looks great!" I cried out to keep her from waiting any longer for a response.

"You really think so?" she questioned.

"Yes, this is better than my mom has ever done!" I promised.

"Thank you, thank you very much," she said, in an artificially deep tone of voice.

"I better get in the shower," I told her, scratching at my neck that was covered in hair.

"While you are in there, I will sweep up the hair," said Erica, dashing out the door to find a vacuum. *Does she even know where we keep it?* I went into the bathroom, grabbed a towel and hung it on the towel rack.

I stripped off and hopped into the shower. The water was cold! It took a while, but it finally warmed up. I just did a quick rinse, no shampoo or conditioner, just a rinse to get the hair cuttings off my neck and shoulders.

I dried off with a towel and put on clean clothes. I could hear Erica using the vacuum. When I left the bathroom, she was just turning it off. Mom was sitting on my bed, looking concerned.

She looked at my hair and gasped.

"Erica, you are right, you did a wonderful job!" Mom said with relief and left.

"Even Mom likes it. You did such a great job," I said to Erica.

"Thanks! While you were in the shower, I called my mom. She is on her way over."

"Why?" I asked, wondering if I had done something to upset her.

"I have homework, and I have to check on my pets. It is getting kind of late," she answered. I nodded.

"Where did Eric go?" I asked, looking around. I had completely forgotten about him.

"He left the room before I cut your hair," Erica answered.

"Oh, well, ok, what are you going to do about your hair?" I asked.

"Mom will cut it for me."

"Ok, so, when will your mom get here?" I asked. Just then we heard a honk.

We raced out to the kitchen and peered out a window. A gruff looking lady stood there with her car door opened. Eric stood next to her.

"That is my mom, bye!" she cried, hugging me.

"Bye, see you at school!" I said. She left to go get into the car, and I went back to my room.

Chapter 8: Walk in the Woods

THE NEXT DAY, I woke up early and took the time to read some more of the Hatchet book and helped Mom fix breakfast.

"How has school been?" She asked. I shrugged. There were defiantly pros & cons.

"I received an e-mail from your teacher that you have been passing notes in class." I scowled. *Mr. Hopkins is making me miserable at home now, too?*

"Mom, I didn't write the note! I was just passing it on for a boy behind me. I even told the teacher that!" I exclaimed, exasperated that Hopkins had told on me to my mom. It wasn't like I really did anything bad.

The boy behind me should have been punished, not me. Maybe Hopkins e-mailed his parents, too. At least Hopkins didn't send me to detention. I wondered about the boy.

"I believe you, and even if you did write a note and pass it on, I wouldn't be mad at you. I passed my fair share of notes when I was in school." I had to smile at that: my own mother passing notes in class.

"Really?"

"Yep, but still, if you ever do pass notes, don't get caught." She winked at me. "But I still really want you to pay attention in school. It's important." She stared at me sternly.

"Have you ever seen me get a bad grade?" I ask her. She nodded.

"You got a B- in history last year, remember?" I rolled my eyes.

"Ok, once, in my least favorite subject, I got a bad grade." We laughed and then the twins ran into the kitchen.

"Food!" they cried.

***

Will walked into the classroom. Unlike the first time I saw him, he looked shy. I waved to him and he returned the gesture.

Next to me, on the right, was the only empty desk in the classroom. He sat down beside me, pulling his books out. I had noticed when he came in, he had been carrying a lunchbox.

"Will, just so you know, you need to put your backpack in the closet at the back of the room and your lunchbox on the cart on by the door."

"Thanks," he said.

Hopkins came into the room just as Will was sitting back down.

"Ah, Will, I see you found your seat. Why don't you come up here and introduce yourself to the class?" Will didn't move. Finally, he sighed and walked up to the front of the class.

"Everyone, this is Will. He is a new student. Will, tell us something about you," Mr. Hopkins said. Will hesitated then spoke up.

"Um, I just moved here from New York," he said.

"Anything else?" Mr. Hopkins asked, almost as though he were interrogating Will.

"I like to play soccer, and I like to camp," Will said. Then before Hopkins could interrogate him any longer, he sat down.

***

Erica and I sat together at lunch. I spotted Will struggling to find a place to sit down. I waved to him. We had seats to spare. He either didn't see me or pretended he didn't. He sat with some other boys a few tables over.

"Who was that?" Erica asked, turning her head to look at him.

"Oh, that is Will. He just moved from New York." Erica squinted up her face.

"Why?" Erica asked. I answered with a shrug.

"I have no clue." Erica and I finished our meals and then headed out to the park. We decided to play soccer again.

Will was there organizing teams, putting a stop to the disaster of a soccer team we had had before; if you could even call it a soccer team. It was just a bunch of kids running and kicking a ball!

Since we didn't have jerseys, he found another way to identify the teams. Half the kids had hats on, the other half didn't. Erica and I ended up on the hatless team. We lost by a lot without Will on our side.

After school, the twins and I decided we wanted to take a walk in the woods. Mom told us we could as long as we didn't go far. She warned us to watch where we were going, so we wouldn't get lost. She also reminded us that there could be snakes.

After she dowsed us with bug spray, I grabbed my camo backpack and filled it with stuff like the first-aid kit, a bottle of water, a few granola bars, a banana, three peanut butter sandwiches, a rag, binoculars, and a couple of Ricolas.

The twins and I crossed the creek for the first time with one graceful leap. Ken didn't make it all the way across and soaked one of his tennis shoes luckily he didn't seem to mind.

We had such a blast weaving in and out of trees and chasing each other. We found a wonderful climbing tree. We spent time climbing it before continuing. Everything was great until I whispered to myself, "Where am I? Where are we! We are lost!"

"What did you say, Morgan?" asked Sara.

"Guys, I don't know where we are! We are lost!"

"Don't be silly!" said Ken, looking around nervously.

"We can't be lost!" said Sara, also looking scared.

"Guys! I am serious! I am completely clueless about which way the house is! So, unless you know which way to go, we are doomed!"

I started freaking out inside my head. I didn't want to show it though; I tried to stay calm for the twin's sakes. Sara burst out in tears and started running, just randomly!

"Sara! Where are you going? Come back!" We chased her. Finally, I caught up with her. I grabbed her by the shoulders, shaking her gently.

"Sara! We have to stick together! Stay with me; I am the only one with water." Ken started cursing; he was crying now and yelling over and over a word he shouldn't even know, let alone use.

"Ken! Stop it! We have to stay calm. You are using up all your water by crying so many tears."

The twins kept hiccupping, but had stopped crying. I was scared, too, probably even more than the twins. I knew what could happen to us. If we had gotten all the way back into the endless, undeveloped Hoosier National Forest, we would never be found!

"I want Mommy!" yelled Sara, sitting down in the leaves.

"I know! Calm down! We will find our way back, I know it! Here, listen. I know a neat trick that most people don't. I learned it as a Girl Scout. We just need to find an acorn, and we will be able to find our way home." The twins brightened, they truly had total faith in me now. They thought that I would be able to guide us back with only an acorn, which wasn't entirely true.

We looked around for acorns. At last Sara found one. "Here! I got it! Here!" She handed it to me. I pulled off the cap while the twins watched me, fascinated, never questioning me. I placed my thumbs in special places on the cap and blew into it. It produced an ear-splitting whistle.

"How will that help us get home?" asked Ken.

"Someone may hear it and come looking for us," I explained. I sat down against a tree and blew again. The twins covered their ears this time. I kept blowing until the acorn cap was too wet with spit to make a sound.

"Morgan, no one has come!" shrieked Sara.

"Don't worry, someone heard it," I said, not so sure.

"Ah-h-h!" screamed Sara.

"WHAT!" I yelled, startled.

"A-uh, uh, s-s-s-s-s-SNAKE!" Sara screamed. It was somewhat concealed under a log.

"It's a snake! Co-o-o-l!" said Ken and picked up a stick. He began poking the snake with it.

"Ken stop! That is a copperhead snake! It is extremely poisonous and can kill you with one bite," I cautioned, pulling Ken away.

"Like a zombie?"

"Yes, only you won't turn into a snake if you are bit. Snakes are more afraid of us than we are of them, but we will still stay away anyways. If you scare it too much, it will strike!" I grabbed Sara and Ken's hands and dragged them away, slowly. Ken threw his stick, like a spear, at the snake and yelled....

"DIE!" The stick barely missed the snake, and it jumped

when the stick landed next to it. It sped away from us and disappeared from sight under some leaves.

"You guys have to be more careful if you want to survive!" I shouted at them.

"You make it sound like we will be out here a long time!" said Sara and started hiccupping again.

"Sara! Don't cry, and if it makes you feel better, I think we may be found by tomorrow."

"Tomorrow? No! Does that mean we are sleeping out here all night?"

"Probably," I replied.

"No! We can't!" moaned Sara. *I need to find a way to calm them down, think, think…! That is it!*

"Sara, Ken, it is getting late. You don't want the wild beasts that come out at night to get you, do you? They are vicious, but they can't see or smell very well, so they will stalk out whatever is loudest. They hate whistling though. So as long as you're with me, you will be safe." That was a lie of course, but I needed them to calm down. The twins covered their mouths to muffle out the faint hiccups.

"Whistle, Morgan!" whispered Sara. So I whistled. The twins and I scuttled around to try and find a comfy resting place. Finally we gave up. What were we looking for? A bed? Good luck with that!

We stopped at a flat place at the edge of a ravine and piled up as many leaves as possible with our hands. I took off my backpack and set it next to us. We curled up, snug on our makeshift bed. The twins asked me to whistle one last time. We were all so tired. We fell straight to sleep despite the mosquitos swarming around us. I couldn't believe how fast the twins fell asleep! They had been the ones worried that they would be dragged off and eaten by some vicious, rabid creature during the night.

***

"Ah-h-h-h-h-h-h-h-h-h!" I heard a scream, while I was sleeping. The noise made me startle awake. I looked around; Sara was gone!

Chapter 9: Which Way Out?

KEN WAS STILL FAST ASLEEP. For a brief moment, I believed the made-up story I had told the twins about the vicious creatures. Maybe Sara had been dragged away! But then I remembered that there was nothing in these woods that would be interested in human flesh for a meal.

"Sara!" I shouted, which woke Ken up, too.

"Morgan! Help me!" she started weeping. I could tell she was fairly close. Thank goodness, it was morning, so I didn't have to look for her in the pitch black. I got up from the damp pile of leaves to search for her.

"It's wet. Did it rain?" asked Ken; he was still half asleep.

"It is the dew," I said and started looking around for Sara.

"Sara! Where are you?!"

"Down in the creek!" she yelled, which made me realize what had happened to her. She had rolled down the hill, into the ravine.

I looked down the ravine we had been sleeping by. There was Sara, grasping to a tree so she wouldn't fall back down. She had already made it half way back up; her hair was a mess. She was dripping wet from the creek, and bloody. Very bloody! I couldn't figure out how she had rolled all the way down without being stopped by one of the many trees.

"Sara! I am coming! I slowly worked my way down to where she was by grabbing one tree at a time. The roots sticking out of the side of the bank acted as great steps, until one broke. I lost my balance and tumbled down the rest of the way, screaming.

"Morgan! NOOOO!" cried Sara, grabbing for me as I passed by her. She was, of course, too weak to keep me from tumbling the rest of the way down. She plummeted down with me.

Only my face landed in the creek, but Sara wasn't so lucky. She was fully in the water again! So much for my help! We dragged ourselves out of the creek. I stood there on the slope and looked down at myself; I was muddy and bloody like Sara now. I was also bruised everywhere and had too many scrapes to count.

We started back up the ravine. I had to clutch each little tree that I came across to keep from tumbling back down into the creek. One of the tree limbs, that I had grasped, snapped. I almost lost my balance, but I regained it by grabbing onto another small tree.

"We made it!" Sara cried, as we flung ourselves up onto the flat area. I dragged the twins a good distance till we were far from the edge of the ravine.

"Stay here!" I said sternly, so they knew I meant business. They didn't question me as I walked back to the makeshift bed. I grabbed my backpack and carried it to Sara. I rummaged through it until I found my first-aid kit, the water, and the rag. Sara was still crying, softly, as I dabbed at her wounds. Then Sara squealed in pain.

"Sara! It will get infected if I don't clean it, so stay still." She clenched her teeth as I added Neosporin and Band-Aids to the boo-boos. I used gauze on the larger ones.

"It hurts!" Sara whimpered. When I was done, she looked like a mummy, and I think she felt like one, too. When I finally had time to work on myself, there were only enough BAND-AIDS and gauze for a few of my ouchies.

That meant I wasn't as mummified as Sara. I was too afraid to use the rag I had used on Sara since it had her blood. I didn't want her blood in my system. *Good thing I read that survival of the fittest handbook last year!* I thought to myself: *Otherwise, I would be clueless on this stuff.*

"I need to go to the bathroom!" whined Ken. I had almost forgotten he was there; he had been so silent.

"Go behind that tree." I instructed.

"But I have to do number two! I need a REAL bathroom!" he exclaimed, looking anxious.

"Oh," I said. What did the Indians do? They had to go to the restroom somewhere! *Think! Think!* I scanned my brain and then remembered that the Indians used leaves for toilet paper.

"Ken, go in that bush over there and wipe with leaves." *I will save you some of the disgusting details about how Ken went about his business and skip to after the deed was done.*

"Done!" he cried. He bounded back to where Sara and I were sitting.

"I am hungry!" said Sara. I reached into my backpack and pulled out the granola bars. We each ate one and took tiny sips of water, so it wouldn't run out too soon.

"What now?" Sara asked.

"We wait and whistle," I said. We found some more acorns and put the caps to our lips. Sara and Ken made a pathetic little blowing noise, but my cap made the clearest whistle, yet.

Ken threw down his cap. "I can't do it!" he complained.

"Me either!" said Sara and mimicked Ken by throwing her acorn lid down, too.

"Here. I will show you," I said and showed them how to place their thumbs over the lid.

After I showed Sara how to do it, she had made a tiny whistle sound on her first try! She cried, "I did it!" This made Ken even madder. His twin sister could do it, but he couldn't!

Finally, after lots of determination and multiple tries, both of the twins were great whistlers.

"Welcome to the whistling club!" I said. We went through many different acorn caps until we couldn't stand to whistle any longer.

"Let's walk around and try to find home," said Sara. I agreed with her, and we left our camp. I scratched at my bug bites the whole time and whistled a bit.

"Sara, this is no use. We might just be walking farther and farther away." That is when I saw it! The savior, our savior! The ticket home! There in front of us was a tree, THE tree.

"Guys! I found home!" I yelled. There was the tree we had spent half-an-hour climbing the day before. I couldn't believe it!

"Yes!" cried the twins. I started running towards our creek. I couldn't see it yet, but I knew it was coming up. The twins ran as fast as possible, trying to keep up.

"Wait! Morgan! Wait up! Wait for us!" they cried. I knew they would stay fairly close to me, so I kept going full speed, peeking back every once in a while to make sure they weren't too far behind.

"There it is! The creek! I see it!" I cried and leaped over it. I was back in our yard. There was Mom sitting on our back deck. I ran for her, and she spotted me. She got up and ran, too.

"Oh thank goodness!" she cried. The twins emerged from the woods and dashed up to Mom.

"Mommy!" cried Sara. She grasped Mom around her waist.

"Sara! Morgan! You guys look like mummies! What happened to you?" She pried us off her. I looked down at my feet.

"We rolled all the way down a ravine! I was really bloody, so Morgan mummified me," explained Sara. I was surprised she knew the word mummified.

"I am so glad you three are alright! Ken, you didn't get hurt too, did you?" He shook his head. "Good! Ok, I will be right back. I need to call your father. We have been worried sick! And Morgan, don't think you're off the hook! How could you? We looked for you all night!"

She disappeared into the house. I felt like I was going to vomit. Mom had never gotten really mad at me before. She had never used that 'you're-in-big-trouble voice' on me, only the twins! It wasn't even my fault! I didn't try to get lost! She came back and the twins leeched onto her sides.

"Why aren't the twins in big trouble?" I asked.

"You are older, that means you were in charge, you

should have paid more attention to your surroundings," said Mom. That one really stabbed my heart. Deep inside I knew she was right, but I couldn't admit it.

"Morgan, come here and hug me, too," said Mom, holding out an arm. I couldn't resist. I embraced her with a warm hug and shed a few embarrassing tears. From behind Mom, I saw a few police officers and Dad come out of the woods.

"Dad!" cried Ken and Sara. They raced out to him and hugged him, tightly.

"I was so worried about you! You about gave your mother a heart attack when you didn't come home for dinner," said Dad. I stayed up on the deck. I was too ashamed! Dad and the twins walked back to the house, they climbed up the steps to the deck, and Dad whispered something to Mom.

"Sara, Ken, don't go inside. You are both too dirty!"

"Aw! Do we have to take a shower?" Ken asked.

"Yes, you will, but let your father hose you off, first." Dad walked out into the yard with the twins and turned the hose on them.

"Now Morgan, what happened?! Can we not trust you

anymore?! I am grateful you are ok, but geesshh! Tell me what happened," said Mom.

I pulled my backpack off, since it was beginning to weigh me down. I set the backpack on the warm concrete and told Mom my story:

"Well, we were having fun walking through the woods when we found this awesome climbing tree; it was a beach tree. After we played on that for a half an hour, we continued on. Then I realized I hadn't been....well, I hadn't been..." I couldn't spill the words. Actually saying it, I could tell how irresponsible it would sound.

Finally, I made myself spill it... "I hadn't been paying attention to the surroundings, and we got lost. I blew on acorn lids to make a whistle, but you guys couldn't hear us. When it got dark, we made a bed of leaves and went to sleep."

"How did Sara and you get so hurt?!" asked Mom.

"I was about to get to that. I woke up to her screaming this morning, and I didn't see her anywhere! Turns out, in her sleep, she had rolled down into the ravine and scratched herself up. By the time I figured out where she was; she was on her way back up. I went down to help her, but then I fell, too. She grabbed onto me, but she fell again! We both rolled back down the ravine. We had to work very hard at it, but we finally escaped."

"I am just glad you are ok; go have Dad hose you off now."

I took off my shoes and ran into the yard. Dad gave me a long, one-armed hug, while spraying the twins. "Ok! Spray me!" *BURR!* It was cold; the twins had gotten all the warm water. The twins started a game.

"Abandon ship! Mayday! Mayday! Mayday! We are going down! Water is getting in the ship!" Ken cried.

"Captain! What do we do now?" Sara asked Ken, flailing her arms and running in tight, small circles under the hose.

"We will d-r-o-w-n!" I cried.

"Everyone, abandon ship!" yelled Captain Ken.

"What should we do about the supplies?! All that gold we have under deck! We will lose it!" I yelled.

"Our lives mean more!" Dad yelled, joining in the fun.

"No! My third mate is right! We worked so hard to steal that gold! Sara, grab a bucket! Morgan, find something to plug the hole with!"

Sara started scooping with an imaginary bucket, and I pretended to stuff the hole with an imaginary rag. Mom turned off the water.

"You're making mud!" she cried. The twins and I celebrated.

"We plugged the hole! The gold is saved!

***

Mom was right; she wasn't letting me off that easy. After a long talk, an hour of back-breaking chores, and a timeout, she was finally finished making my life miserable. Let's just say, I won't be in the woods for a while.

Chapter 10: Hi, Grandma! Hey, Grandpa!

THE NEXT MORNING my mom and dad, the twins, and I were eating waffles, when we heard someone pull in the driveway.

“I wonder who is here. I didn’t invite anyone,” said Mom, standing up to peer out the window.

“Oh, my gosh! Grandma and Grandpa are here!” said Mom. I dropped my fork, and it clattered onto the plate.

“Grandma and Grandpa are dead!” The twins said, stating the obvious.

“Sara, Ken, Morgan, come outside, these are your other grandparents!” The twins and I raced outside.

An elderly couple struggled out of their truck. I couldn’t believe it! It really was my other grandparents. I hadn’t seen them since I was 5! I barely remembered them, but here they were. They had brought a pull-behind RV and presents.

Grandma was an overly skinny lady that looked like she was about to be swept off her feet from the wind. She was in good shape, though, for her age. She had brown hair with gray streaks that fell down to the middle of her back. Without the wrinkles, she would look like she was in her mid-fifties.

Grandpa, on the other hand, looked twice his age. It looked like he hadn't exercised in ages, with his round pot-belly. *I will never forget his beard. It always had food stuck in it from his last meal.* As he approached, sure, enough, I could see the tidbits of food stuck throughout it.

"Who are you?" asked the twins, scowling up at them.

"We are your grandparents!" the lady explained.

"Our grandparents died!" said Sara. They just couldn't accept the concept that they had another set of grandparents.

"We are your *other* grandparents," said the guy, like he was bored out of his mind. I was still in a bit of a shock that they were here. No postcard, phone-call, or e-mail that I knew of saying: 'Hey this is Grandma Sharron and

Grandpa Rick. We are coming to your house.'

"Mom, Dad, why didn't you say you were coming?" Mom asked them. I could tell she was as stunned as the rest of us.

"Well, in your e-mail, you said to come down whenever we liked," Sharron smiled.

"Yes, but I thought you would call first!" Mom exclaimed.

"Let's leave that behind us. We have presents!" Sharron handed a large wrapped present to both of the twins.

"Careful with those, keep them upright."

"Yay!" they cried and ran into the house. Sharron chuckled and walked over to me, "…and this is for you," she said, as she handed over a rectangular box.

"Thank you! Uh … Grandma," I said and stood there for a very awkward moment. I wanted to run inside like the twins, but I thought that would be rude.

"I like your shoes," I said, to find an excuse to look down. I didn't want to look at her eyes anymore. They were bulgy and had many different colors in them.

"Well, are you going to hug your Grandma?!" asked Sharron, spreading her arms, preparing to give me a hug. I set down my package and hugged her. Finally, the awkward moment was over when the twins clambered outside, yelling and screaming.

"Thank you! Thank you! Thank you!" They cried and took turns hugging both Sharron and Rick.

"What did Grandma get you?" Mom asked.

"I got a lizard that changes color!" Ken exclaimed, mesmerized.

"I got a parrot!" cried Sara. "It said, 'Hi Sara! You look lovely today!'"

"Mom! You got them pets! We don't have time for pets!" Mom complained.

"Sure you do! You are a housewife!" retorted Sharron. Mom rolled her eyes; I could tell she was upset. *Who wouldn't be, her parents who she hadn't seen for years show up on her doorstep, hands her a few pets, insults her, and says…*

"Let's get to the point, we need a place to stay, we are broke." All of us, except the twins, gasped. All the twins cared about were their presents.

"We are going to play with our pets!" said the twins. They dashed back into the house.

"What are you saying?" asked Dad, scratching his head; *he did this when he was nervous.*

"We were wondering if there was room for us here in your new home."

Mom and Dad whispered for a bit. Mom sighed.

"I guess you can sleep in Jack's office." My dad, Jack, didn't look too happy about that.

"Oh, thank you!" said Grandma, almost like the twins would. Grandpa stayed quiet except for a little murmur that I couldn't make out. He opened up the RV and lugged out two over-sized suitcases and one small one.

"Whoa, whoa! Hang on a minute, how long are you staying? This is only temporary, right? Just so you can get back on your feet?" asked Mom, staring at the bags.

"Well, I don't know. It could be weeks or months, even...." *Don't say years; don't say years*, I begged inside my head.

"...years. I don't know though, with your money you could probably get us an apartment, that would be the best way to repay us," said Grandma.

"Repay you for what? I already paid you back for my schooling," said Mom.

"We cared for you for seventeen years, buying you clothes, food and keeping a roof over your head." I still couldn't believe what I was hearing. I hoped when I grew up I wouldn't have to buy my parents an apartment.

Mom threw aside that last comment and questioned, "How did this happen anyway! How did you go bankrupt?"

Grandma ushered my mom and dad over into a little huddle that looked like a football team deciding on what play to use. I guess Grandma didn't want me to know. I saw that opportunity, so I picked up my present and ran inside, careful not to shake the package, just in case there was an animal inside. I didn't see any holes punched into it, and it was fairly small, so I decided it probably didn't hold an animal.

I carried it down the hall and into my room. Setting it on the bed carefully, I started to rip it open. Inside was a polished wooden box with my name engraved into it. If Grandma and Grandpa were broke, how could they afford all these glamorous things: the RV, a box specially engraved, pets that could talk and change colors?

I shook the box gently and found out that there was something inside. I tried to open the box, but I couldn't figure it out. Mom yelled something from outside my door.

"WHAT?!" I yelled back.

"School! YOU ARE LATE FOR SCHOOL!!!" Mom yelled.

"Oh! I will hurry!" I rustled about, brushing my hair in my bathroom, throwing on a couple hair clips to keep the hair away from my eyes, grabbing my backpack. I ran down the hall and into the kitchen.

"In the car, the car!" Mom yelled. Dad was nowhere in sight; he must of left for work. I sprinted out the door and got into the car. Then I remembered my Grandparents; where were they?

Mom rushed the twins into the back of our Kia and strapped them in.

"No! No!" they screamed. "I want to say bye to Mango Bango!" Sara said, scratching Mom. Mango Bango? Who the heck was Mango Bango? *Must be a doll.*

"Sara! We are going to be late for school!"

"We?" I questioned.

"You, I MEANT YOU, KIDS!" she yelled. The twins quieted down after hearing her yell. She slammed the door and hopped into the driver's seat.

***

I pulled the twins out of the car and dragged them onto the path. There were no kids on the playground, no supervisors, just us. I hauled the twins to their classroom and sprinted off to mine. I knew I shouldn't run, but I was in a hurry.

"Whoa, there! Where are you going in such a hurry?" I turned and saw that I was staring up into the eyes of the principal.

"I, I, it is just I, was late for school, and I was trying to make up time."

"Ok, but no more running!" I nodded and started back for my class.

***

At recess all the girls were playing soccer, so I went to join them, since Erica was nowhere to be seen. They were playing a game to solve a bet.

The bet was: girls are just as athletic as boys. If the girls win, the boys have to be nice to the girls for a week. If the boys win, the girls have to get pudding for them in the cafeteria every day for a week, so they can have extra.

Typical boys, all they think about is food and sports. I played the best I could. I only made one goal. The boys' team had a great goalie.

Will wasn't there, so that helped the girls' team. Half of the girls were ruthless, as tough as the boys, the other half… let's just say, not so much. They were 'girly', girls. But there were some weak boys too.

Sadly the game ended in a tie when the bell rang. It was 23 to 23. I guess that is better than losing.

By the end of the day, I was very ready to go home. So were the twins. They were anxious to play with their new pets. On the bus they had sat behind me, and they kept poking me in the head. When we got home, I was so annoyed by them, that at first, I didn't notice the mess in the house.

But once the twins left me, I gasped. All around me

were piles of boxes. They were strewn everywhere.

Where had all these come from? Then I remembered Grandma was here. Supposedly, she went to numerous therapists because of her hording addiction. She wasn't one of those crazy hoarders that couldn't even throw out a dirty diaper, but she sure did horde clothes.

I glanced out the window and there was a moving van parked outside. Two beefy men were lugging in the heavy cardboard boxes…more boxes!

"Grandma! Where are all these boxes coming from?" Grandma hustled in from the next room.

"Hmm?"

"Where did all these boxes come from?!" I repeated.

"Oh, that. Since I am poor now, I couldn't pay the bill for the storage unit," said Grandma, as if it was perfectly normal to have a thousand boxes of clothes tucked away in a storage unit.

Mom isn't going to be happy about this," I said. Grandma smirked.

"I already talked to her, she said it was alright. I might have forgotten to mention how many boxes there were, but I think she will understand. There are only 15 boxes."

"If I know Mom, she won't be pleased," I told Grandma, staring at the big box next to me.
"What is in all of them?"

"Clothes mostly," she replied. I couldn't believe it. No wonder they were poor. Who wouldn't be after buying enough clothes to give a shirt to every person in America?

I just shook my head with wonder and walked to my room. Sara and Ken walked through the door shortly after.

"Is this the house of April Gill?" asked Sara in her most adult-sounding voice.

"Why, yes, it is! How may I help you?" I asked, playing along.

"We were wondering if you have seen this dog," said Ken, holding up a blank piece of paper.

"Why! Yes, I have. He ran straight through my yard just the other day!" I said, in a southern accent.

"Thank you, Ma'am!" Sara cried and slammed the door

as she ran off.

I picked up the box with my name engraved on it from my grandparents and shook it slightly again. I wondered how it opened! Then I turned it over. On the underside, there was a picture of an elephant. It had its trunk pointed up to the sky.

Taking the box, I walked down the hall and into the living room where Grandma was opening up one of her boxes. I asked her how to open my box.

"Oh, right! Let me show you." She grasped the box and put one finger on the top right corner and the other finger on the bottom left corner. Then she gently pulled out.

She handed the box to me, and I looked inside. There was a little necklace with a globe charm. The globe looked like the earth, and it had a clasp. I opened the earth and it sang.

"Be happy! Don't worry now, o-o-o-o, o-o-o-o o-o-o-o-o-o-o, don't worry. O-o-o-o-o-o, be happy! O-o-o-o-o-o, don't worry, be happy!" it sang. Next, came a recording of Grandmas voice:

"We love you, from Grandma and Grandpa. Don't forget, you can achieve anything if you only try!" It turned off automatically. I looked up at Grandma, speechless!

"Thanks!" was all I could manage to say. I hugged her and went to hide my treasure in my room. I didn't want the twins taking it! That reminded me. Where were the twins? I searched and searched till I found a trail of bird seed and followed it down to the closet under the basement stairs.

"MORGAN!!!" Sara shouted, happily.

"Hey," I said.

"Morgan, look at what Sara's bird can do!" Ken exclaimed. I looked over and there was Sara's bird.

"Polly wants a cracker! Sara, hello, Sara! My! Ken you look fine! Morgan, Morgan, Morgan! Let me out! I love you, Sara! I am Polly. Nice to meet you! Hello. Sara, my name is Polly!" it screeched.

"It said my name… and both of yours!" I exclaimed, impressed.

"Yeah, isn't it cool?" Ken said, again.

"Yeah, isn't it cool?" cried the bird.

"Stop copying me!" yelled Ken.

"Stop copying me!" squawked the bird.

"Uh!" Ken cried, in frustration.

"Not my fault," said the bird. I had to laugh at that last comment. It was hilarious. Next, we let the bird out of the cage. We let it flap around the closet, sit on our shoulders, sit on our heads, and talk. It was a great, well-trained bird.

"Sara, what else can it say?" I asked.

Sara answered, "Get away! I want some water, no more crackers for Polly, me stuffed!"

"That is all it has said?" I asked.

"Yep, that is it!" Sara said.

"What did you name it? Polly?" I asked. Sara shook her head.

"No, I named it Mango Bango," she replied. *Oh, so that is who Mango Bango is*! I thought. I went back upstairs again and there were Mom and Grandma arguing. I didn't listen to what they were discussing, but I guessed it had something to do with all the boxes stacked around the house.

"Morgan! There you are! We have to plan your birthday!" She huffed, "It is in only more five days! I planned part of it and sent out the invitations. Here is what I thought we could do. First, you play in the back yard, and then you have cake and presents, and after that we can go to the aquarium!"

"That sounds great, did you invite Erica?"

"Yep, hey do you want me to invite Will?" I nodded.

"Sure," I answered and ran down the hall and into my room. In my room I found Ken and Sara sitting on my bed, innocently.

"What did you do now?!" I asked.

Chapter 11: Birthday Bash

"WAKE UP! GET UP! You don't want to miss your party, do you?" Sara and Ken yelled, into my ear. It seemed as though I had just gone to bed. How could time pass so quickly, I thought to myself?

Then I remembered. I was giving the twins the silent treatment. They had gone into my bedroom five days ago. The day Grandma and Grandpa showed up; they broke into my specially engraved box. They broke the box so it wouldn't close right! Luckily, I had caught them before they broke the necklace, too, but I was still fuming.

I sat up and pretended they weren't there. I had assured them I wouldn't talk to them till my birthday party started. They seemed like they were getting anxious.

"Morgan, please talk to us! We are sorry," said Sara, but I only made a shooing motion with my hands. They caught the hint and left my room. That was a surprise! Maybe the silent treatment was having some effect on them.

I quickly showered, put on some clothes and the necklace I got from Grandma and Grandpa. I put on a hint of make-up. It was only lip stick, but that was more than nothing. Then I went down for breakfast. I don't know why the twins had said I would be late for my birthday. It didn't start till 1:00 o'clock.

"HAPPY BIRTHDAY!" yelled my whole family while jumping out from behind chairs and under the table.

There were Mom, Dad, Ken, Sara, Uncle John, Uncle Dan, Aunt Lucy, Aunt Ashley, Aunt Jess, Grandma and Grandpa, Cousin Jamie, Cousin Beth, Cousin Elli, Cousin Oliver, Cousin Michael, and last but not least, Cousin Darik.

"SURPRISE," said Ken, Sara and Darik.

"I…thank you. I am speechless! I have never had a surprise birthday before!"

"Now you have!" said Cousin Jamie. I really was speechless. I hadn't seen Jamie, or most of them, since I was a lot younger. Some of them lived in Canada, and some of them lived in Florida. I looked over to the right and there was a pile of gifts. They were stacked high towards the ceiling. That is when it hit me… I am ten! Double digits!

"How are you sweetheart?" Aunt Jess asked.

"Fine, I haven't seen you in forever, or most of you for that matter." There was a long moment of people taking turns hugging me and wishing me happy birthday.

"WHO is ready for some cake?" Mom asked.

She held out a round, triple-layer cake with "HAPPY BIRTHDAY," written in blue icing with beautiful flowers spread over the top. All my cousins, that were younger than me, lunged forward when they saw it. They almost knocked the cake out of my mom's hands. Their parents scolded them and made them wait in line. I got the first piece. It looked even more scrumptious cut than it did before with its icing flowing out from the center.

"Thank you everyone!" I said, just as I stuffed my face with the first bite. The twins were served, and in only a moment, looked so messy with the icing coated on their cheeks, but of course they didn't mind.

After we ate our cake, I opened the presents. I got some great stuff. The little, remote control helicopter, money, and I-pod were my favorite gifts.

The iPod was from my mom and dad, so of course, they just had to get one for both of the twins, case and all. After that, we went out to eat and things started to get interesting. We went to a restaurant called Mr. Gabs, but the twins came along, so trouble would be following soon. They can be so funny, but also annoying at times.

They went straight to the indoor playground with Darik, our 5-year-old cousin. Right away Sara noticed a little space where she could slip in behind the play equipment.

She whispered to Ken, and they snuck through the opening to the back of the equipment. But when they tried to get back through, they couldn't. Sara got stuck.

"AAAAAAAAHHHHHHHHHHHHHH! HELP!!! I am stuck!" Mom rushed over and pulled on her, but it was no use. She would have to go backwards. Sara finally got herself free going backwards, but she was still behind all the equipment. The staff had to cut the netting to let her out. They didn't seem too happy about that. By then everyone had ordered so we waited for our food in an awkward silence.

Finally, Uncle John broke it by saying, "Wow, double digits, huh? That must seem big!" he said to me. I only nodded in reply.

"So how is Dorothy doing?" Mom asked, turning to Jess, trying to start a conversation.

"Ok, but she is in prison for robbery," said Jess, plainly. Dorothy was Jess's now ex-friend. That only made things more awkward. It didn't help that I didn't know what to say.

What do you say to a table of relatives you barely know?

"Is anything interesting happening in Florida?" I asked Dan.

"It is hot and rainy," he responded.

"K," I said, not sure what else I should say.

"How about in Canada?" I asked Jess.

"Same. I got a new car though, an SUV." This had to be the most awkward birthday party, yet. Finally, the food arrived. Steam was drifting from the plates. I nibbled on my fish bites. I was not especially hungry.

The Sill family wasn't that close to one another. When we were finished eating, and the manager had apologized for the unsafe playground equipment, we went home. My cousins and I watched a movie while we waited for the next party to begin.

At one o'clock the first guests arrived: Erica and Eric. Eric rushed to the Ken's room, but Erica stayed with me.

"Where are the other guests?" she inquired.

"They will be here shortly. By the way, why weren't you in school yesterday?" I asked.

"Oh, I had a sore throat and Mom kept me home, just in case, but I am fine now," Erica replied.

Very soon the other kids arrived, and we did all the things Mom had planned. When everyone had gone home except for Erica and Eric, I offered to take Erica into the woods. Surprisingly, Mom and Dad didn't object. I packed up a dinner for us since it was almost 5:00, and we headed off.

"Are there any good climbing trees around?" asked Erica.

"Yep, we have a great one. Just a bit farther," I replied. When we finally got there, Erica quickly sprang up into the tree. I wasn't quite as fast as her. She was, like, part monkey. Once we got high enough that we could see the house, we stopped climbing. We were super high.

"I have never been this high in a tree before," I said.

"I haven't either."

"Do you want to explore the woods some more?" I asked.

"Sure!" So we shimmied down the tree and sprinted over to a ravine. This time I was being careful not to lose my way.

"LOOK!" cried Erica, scooting down the ravine holding onto trees for support.

"What?" I asked, scurrying after her. Then I saw it down at the bottom. There was a whole car down there! *I wonder what is inside!*

Chapter 12: The Old Car

ERICA FLUNG OPEN THE DOOR to the car and jumped in. The car had broken windows, and it was rusty but she didn't seem to care. Inside there was a key sitting on the bench seat.

I hopped in beside her just as she stuck the key into the ignition and turned. I wished I could say "The car works!" but it didn't. It didn't even make a hint of a sound. Who knew how long it had been there.

"Morgan! You know what this means?!!" yelled Erica.

"We found a car?" I asked.

"Yes, that, too, but no. We found our own place! Somewhere no one but us knows about! Our very own secret hide-out!" Erica cried. I knew she was thrilled. So was I. But I felt like I shouldn't keep it a secret.

"Cool," I said.

"Cool? You mean AWESOME!!!"

"Yeah, awesome!" I agreed. Erica and I searched the car for belongings. I found five dollars in quarters, a journal, and a pack of matches.

Erica found a car manual, two dollars in cash, a pack of cigarettes, and a photograph of the woods.

"Read the journal!" Erica said, shaking with excitement

I looked down at the shriveled paper. There it read…

Dear Diary,   Day 1

Today me and my Dad just hanged around the house. He is a drunk so Mom does most of the work.

She is a nurse. Sometimes she is at the hospital 6:00 AM to 10:00 PM at night!!! I wish she could be around more, but I understand. You could basically call her a single mother, she sure doesn't get any help from Dad.

I did a lot of cleanup work today. Scrubbed the toilets, made the beds, and swept the kitchen floor, the basic stuff.

I always help out mom when I can.

Tomorrow I am going over to my friend Jackie's. She is my favorite friend in the world! She knows how I feel too. Her daddy is a drunk. She is almost a year younger than me but more mature. She is fun still.

Oh! Got to go! Mom just got home!

I stopped there and closed the diary.

"Oh, my gosh! We found a diary!" I exclaimed. If we weren't sitting inside the car, I would be jumping up and down.

"I have never found anything that cool before! Well, I guess you found it, not me," said Erica.

"You found the car though! That is pretty cool. I wonder if that girl used to drive in this car! Those cigarettes are probably her dad's! Or Mom's. You know this car looks really old!" I said, trying to cheer her up. She didn't seem like the type to get jealous over something, but I didn't want her to start.

"Yeah, I guess," she said brightening. "That is kind of cool, read some more." After she said that, I opened the book and read out loud.

Dear Diary, Day 2
Jackie came over today. She is so fun. We took our bikes and biked through the woods on my favorite trail. I named the trail Lazy Lucinda Lane after a girl at school.

Jackie also named a trail. It is called Jackie Dr. Then we went to the Old Kindy Thrift Shop and bought some clothes. Mary, my sister, wanted to come but we insisted to Mom that she would only be a drag. Mom finally agreed that it might be better if Mary stayed home.

I closed the book and turned to Erica. "We better head home before my mom gets worried."

"Right, let's get going. We piled our stuff into my backpack and headed home.

***

"MORGAN!!! Hurry! We caught a snake!" Sara screamed, as we emerged from the woods.

"Ah-h-h! A snake! I hate snakes!" Erica screeched, making yuck faces.

"What? You don't like snakes?! I thought you told me you had every type of pet you could get in America!"

"Everything, but snakes! I HATE snakes! They bite and are slimy, and they're yucky!" Erica exclaimed. I was surprised that she liked frogs but not snakes! Frogs are slimier than snakes by a lot, since snakes aren't even slimy. Snakes do bite, that is true, but so do tigers, lions, bears (oh my), some dogs, raccoons, possums, cats, honey badgers, lizards, and probably more. I am sure every person in the world likes at least one of those animals.

Snakes don't bite often either, unlike lions and a few of the others I listed. Snakes only bite for protection, or if they are eating a mouse.

Many people don't realize that snakes are more afraid of us than we are of them. If you step next to one in the woods it will either flee, stay still in fear, or attack.

How would you feel if a big giant who was 50 times your size stomped down next to you and rattled the ground? Would you flee, cower, or attack?

"Come on Sara! Show me that snake you caught!" I said. I followed her to the house. There by the pool deck was an over turned bucket. Ken was sitting on top of it.

"Look! We caught a snake!" Ken called out, still sitting on the upturned pail.

"Can I see it?" I asked him.

"How can we show you without letting the snake escape?"

"Remove the bucket when I say, go! Then I will catch it with my hands," I said.

"Your hands? E-E-K-K-K!" Erica screamed from

behind me. She was a good ten yards away.

"Yes, my hands. If I recognize it as a poisonous snake, I will not grab it, and let it go. If it is a ring neck snake, I will grab and hold it. Go!!!"

Ken raised the bucket to reveal a curled up ring neck snake. I shot my hand out and grabbed it just behind its head. The ring neck swung its body back and forth, trying to escape from my clutches. I held tight, nevertheless.

"May I pet it?" Sara asked putting forth her hand.

"Course, be gentle though," I instructed her.

Ken came up from behind Sara and came to her side mimicking her actions. Erica stayed back, petrified by the snake's bad reputation.

"Erica, you want to try?!" Ken asked, leaping over to her.

"E-E-K-K-K!" Erica said and ran past us up the stairs leading to the pool deck.

"Keep that scaly thing away from me!" Erica howled, cowering and clutching to the railing.

"You afraid?" Sara asked.

"Yes, very, very, terribly afraid!" Erica replied. I pet the snake one time then let it down in the short grass. Snakes despise short grass because they don't feel hidden and protected like they do in tall grass, so it slithered quickly with its head up all the way to the woods.

"Oh, good! It is gone! Finally!" Erica said, slowly descending the stairs.

"Can we go to your room now?" Erica asked.

"Sure, come on." Erica and I raced to my room, and I showed her the box Grandma got me.

"That is s-o-o-o, cool! Too bad the twins broke it!" Erica said and dropped her head.

"Yeah, I know, right? But look at this!" I pulled the necklace out. Then she opened it. Erica listened to the music in awe. We talked for a bit then Erica cried out.

"Where is Eric? I didn't see him with the twins!"

"Relax! Take a chill pill. He is probably in one of the twin's rooms. Let's go look," I said, leading Erica to Ken's room. Sure enough, there he was playing with Ken's Legos.

"Eric, what are you doing in here by yourself?" Erica asked her brother, kneeling down to him.

"Ken is mean! So is Sara!" Eric said, turning away.

"What did they do?" Erica asked, patiently.

"Ken hit me! Sara just laughed! I hate them!" Eric said. I gasped. I couldn't believe it! They hurt Eric, and then they just left him? They were officially bullies!

"Eric, I am so sorry that the twins were mean to you. I will talk to my Mom about it," I told Eric. But really, I was going to say something to the twins. That was not right for them to hit. It was bad enough when they hurt me, let alone a guest. I stomped down the hallway and out the kitchen door. The twins were playing in the backyard.

"Ken! Sara! Come here! Now!!!" The twins skipped merrily up the steps.

"What is it Morgan?" Sara asked, innocently.

"Did you guys hurt Eric?" I asked them. They looked down at their shoes.

"No," said Ken.

"Yes, you did! Ken, you hit him and Sara, you hurt his feelings!" I burst out.

"I want a lawyer!" Sara shouted.

"Too bad! You can't afford one, and I am not going to provide one! You need to go in there and say you are VERY sorry. Or I am telling Mom!" I warned.

"Don't tell, please! Sara begged.

"Yeah! If you tell on us, we will tell on you!" Ken cried out.

"I didn't do anything though!" I said back.

"Yes, you did!" Sara snapped. Both of the twins whispered, trying to think of something they could blame me on.

"What?"

"You, uh, umm, you hit me! I am going to tell Mom!" Ken yelled. I was furious. I didn't hit him! Or Sara! They took off running toward the house.

"Come back here!" I yelled at the twins.

“Na, na-nu-boo-boo! You can’t catch us,” chanted the twins. “O-o-o, you will be in big trouble!” they cried. The twins reached the door before I could catch them and sprang inside. I was right behind them, but I noticed Mom in there cooking, so I stopped running.

“Mommy!” Sara cried, (fake) sobbing.

“Morgan hit Sara!” Ken cried.

“Morgan! Did you?!” Mom asked, not quite yelling. I winced hoping she didn’t notice.

“No! They made that up since I was going to tell you that they hit Eric!” I huffed, annoyed with the whole situation.

“If Eric says that you two hit him, you will be in big trouble!” Mom said, leaving the room. I hope that means she doesn’t believe that I hit Sara.

***

The twins ended up having a time out. They didn’t mind much since the timeout was in their rooms, and Mom had left them unsupervised. As soon as she left they probably jumped up and started playing with their toys.

Erica and Eric didn’t stay much longer. Their mom

picked them up. We rented a movie called "Annie" after eating supper. It was the new version.

I read for an hour afterward and didn't get to bed till 11:30 P. M.

Chapter 13: Sports

THE DAY AFTER MY BIRTHDAY, I asked my mom if I could start sports. She seemed as excited as I was. They had no extracurricular activities at my old school or my new school besides the regular P.E. It was probably time for me to start doing something besides school and hanging around the house.

"Sure, Sweetie! I will have to do some research and find you an instructor, but that isn't a problem! What would you like to try? Basketball? You did that when you were younger. Or tennis, golf, flag football, or umm, volleyball, softball?" Mom asked.

"I will think about it. I have always admired the game of tennis."

"Ok! I will look it up! I bet I could sign you up for some lessons," I was surprised that Mom was making such a big deal out of it. She had asked me before if I wanted to do lessons, and I had never shown interest. I guess it meant more to her than I thought.

Mom searched the web for roughly a half an hour. When she was done she told me she got me a lesson with some girl named Melody Farcraft. It was a half an hour lesson that was going to happen two days from now. I was pretty excited. Grandma took me to the store to look for rackets and balls, while Grandpa stayed home to watch TV, of course.

When we got there I picked out a black racket and a carton of tennis balls. I also got a case of water bottles to put in the fridge.

***

"Hurry up! Come on, come on! Morgan! Grab the water and let's go!" Mom shouted from the garage. I was going to my first tennis lesson. I picked up the water bottle sitting on the counter and dashed out to the garage. There sat our new van. Mom and Dad had recently gone to a restaurant, and the old Kia had broken down. Mom finally admitted that it was time to get a new car.

It was a great van I thought. It had a built-in TV, seven seats, and each of them had their own heating and cooling vent.

I sprang into the van and buckled up in the seat behind Mom. We were running a touch late because, as usual, the twins were up to mischief.

We had gotten all ready, nice and early, about to leave, when BAM! We heard a crash. Mom and I raced to Ken's room to find that Ken had crawled up to the top shelf in his closet, and it had torn out of the wall. He had really hurt himself and was bleeding quite fiercely.

After Mom cleared up that fiasco, Sara had done something worse. She pulled down the attic door rope and had gone up into the attic. She got fiberglass in her hands and needed some first-aid. Mom finally gave up and dumped the situation on Grandma.

"Mom, when is my lesson? How long will it take to get there?" I asked.

"Your lesson is at 5:00 p. m. It will take fifteen minutes to get there," Mom replied. I peeked at the clock. It said it was 4:52 p. m. We were running late for sure!

We finally got there at 5:05 p. m. That was only because Mom ran a stop light and was driving 5 miles an hour over the speed limit.

We ran up to the instructor, and Mom apologized.

"Sorry! Sorry! I know we are late! I am normally the early type, but we had gotten all ready to go but I had to take care of my younger son, who hurt himself. Nothing that a few band aids couldn't fix. So here we are five minutes late!"

"That is alright," said Melody. "I don't have a tight schedule today. I am glad you son wasn't too hurt. Morgan, the tennis court is this way," Melody said, turning to walk in the direction of the court, and she started walking away. Mom shooed me on, so I followed.

"So, Melody, what do you want me to call you, Mel, Melody, Mrs. Farcraft, or Ms. Farcraft?" I asked. Melody paused for a moment.

"Most of my students call me Mrs. Farcraft, but you may call me Melody or Mel. Mrs. Farcraft makes me sound like an uptight, old lady!" Melody said, smiling. I could tell she was the type who tried to keep things light by being humorous.

We arrived at the court. We set our extra supplies (balls, a racket, and water bottles) on the bench. Melody went to one side, so I went to the other. Then she went into teaching mode.

"Ok, Morgan. To start out, I am going to hit this ball to

you. All I want you to do is hit it. It doesn't matter where it goes. Just hit it with your racket."

Melody swung a light one to me. I ran forward hitting it before it could bounce. The ball flew into the sky! Then it came down in the parking lot.

"Let me rephrase what I said earlier. Hit it, but try to keep it inside the fence. Also, let it bounce once before you hit it. Alright, let's try!" She hit another ball, and I missed it, just barely though. I nipped it on the tip of my racket.

"That is alright! You are a beginner. You aren't expected to hit it every time! Eye on the ball! Ready?" Melody said. I nodded. Another ball came whizzing at me.

I hit the ball and it actually went back to my instructor! *This is fun!* I thought.

She hit it and it came back! I hit it again, but it shot back into the air! *Oh, no. Not again!* It just missed leaving the fence and bounced off it. It ricocheted, heading back to Melody. She ran and swung her racket. It came hurtling back. I closed my eyes as I swung the racket and missed.

"Very good! Wonderful! Quick tip though. Don't close your eyes. It is harder to see the ball that way." She winked at me. Then instead of staying on her side and hitting another ball to me, she came around the net to my side of the court.

She grabbed my racket and guided it like I was hitting a ball. "You want your racket to be open. That way you have a good area to hit the ball with," said my coach, adjusting my grip on the racket.

"There! Perfect!" Now make sure when you come through that you try to hit right here every time." She pointed to the middle of the racket.

"Another thing is, when the ball is on your left, change your racket over to your left side instead of trying to run to it." Melody said, grabbing the racket and holding it out to her left.

"Those shots will be tougher at first since you are right-handed, but after a while it will become natural. You are right-handed, correct?" I nodded.

Melody went back to her side of the net and picked up another ball from a big basket behind her. She threw the ball in the air and hit it to me. It bounced and was going to go over my head. But I stopped it with my racket and it flew forward straight.......into the net across the middle of the court.

"Ahhh!" I breathed out, bummed.

"Don't get too frustrated! It is only a game and this is your first day with lessons. Alright, ready, set, go!" The ball hurtled down to the concrete surface scraping the ground. It bounced up straight for me. It was going to hit my head. I ducked and waited for the ball to pass. I didn't even go for it with my racket.

"Sorry! I didn't mean to hit you!" Coach called, grimacing.

"That is alright! You just missed me anyhow," I replied, shaking off to loosen up.

"Let's pick up a few of these balls before they get in our way," said Melody, spinning the racket in her hand.

***

After the lesson, Mom took me for a mother- daughter lunch. We went to a restaurant. I didn't really care for the batter on the fried fish, but I didn't make a comment to Mom about it.

"Are you looking forward to meeting your new baby sister?" Mom asked, setting down her fork.

"I guess; I just hope she isn't as troublesome as the

twins." I replied, wiping my mouth with a napkin.

"Yeah, so do I. What name did you like the best again?" Mom asked.

"Well, I thought of a new name. It is really pretty: Karenna Lee Sill. It has a lot of nick names too: Karen, Enna, Kary, Rena, Rene, and maybe more," I said, while Mom pondered the name.

"Yeah, that has a bit of a ring to it. I know that having the middle name be Lee is traditional on my side of the family, but I kind of would rather she be named something different like Kathleen or Maureen."

"So it would be Karenna Kathleen or Karenna Maureen? I don't know… I like Karenna Lee better," I replied, biting a crispy, French fry in half.

"All three sound good I think, but not together. Karenna is too much like Kathleen," Mom replied, talking a sip of her cola.

"Why are you having pop, Mom? You never drink pop!" I exclaimed. Mom hadn't had pop since I was born that I could remember.

"I have been craving it since I became pregnant with Karenna," Mom replied, plainly. "That is a good name,

Morgan. I like it."

After finishing up our meal, Mom paid so we could leave.

When I got home I opened up the journal from the car in the forest.

Mary is ok but I am around her a lot so I don't want her around all the time.

Mary is 6 and is in 1st grade. She is sharp though. She should be in third grade in my opinion.

Too bad the school won't allow her to skip a grade or two. It is probably no use though. We move around so much that it would become a pain getting Mary into third grade each time.

Anyway, back to the thrift shop. When me and Jackie got there I bought a skirt, a tank top and a cover up.

Jackie got roughly the same thing.

When we got home Dad was sitting on the couch watching TV...again. It seems like wherever he goes he finds the TV and sits staring blankly sipping from another beer.

My friend Rachel's Dad is hard working, fun, funny, and isn't always in the beer.

She has the best dad ever! So does my other friend Henry. He has a great dad.

At times I find myself jealous but I do love my dad. He didn't always act like this. It happened when Mary turned three I think (somewhere around there anyway). All of a sudden he quit his job, bought a few cases of beer and turned on the TV.

Whenever Mom and Dad are home they argue about him not working. I hope they don't split. I think it would break Mary's heart.

I will write tomorrow, bye!

I feel bad for this girl. I wonder what her name was.

Chapter 14: Mary Who?

"MORGAN!" Grandma called.

"What?!" I yelled back.

"Come here!" I followed the noise. She was in the kitchen making PB&J sandwiches.

"Oh, there you are! What do you want on your PB&J, bananas or raisons?" she asked.

"Neither. I just ate with Mom."

"I know that! But this isn't for now. I want to walk in the woods with you! You can show me around. Maybe you could give me a tour of the treehouse?" Grandma asked.

"Well, ok, I guess I could show you around, just let me

grab my back-pack." I ran to my room and stuffed various items into the sack.

"Coming!" I cried, racing down the hallway to the kitchen.

Grandma was waiting by the kitchen door. We departed, and Grandma asked if she could put the PB&J's in my backpack. I stopped for a moment to let her complete the task.

***

First, we went to the treehouse. "Wow! No wonder the twins like it up here. I am surprised that you don't spend more time here, Morgan!" Grandma exclaimed.

"Yeah, well," I said. Next we went to the forest, but I guided her to the right. That way she wouldn't notice the mysterious car sitting down in the ravine.

"What marvelous woods these are!" Grandma said, staring in awe.

"It is great," I said, looking around. Seeing her face, I finally realized the beauty of the woods. Branches full of lush green leaves were swaying in the gentle breeze. The birds were chipping symphonies, harmonizing with each other. Deer were prancing over fallen trees, and there was the slight sound of water trickling down the ravines.

"Grandma, how did you afford all those gifts you gave me and the twins?" I asked. She turned to me and responded. "Oh, that. An old friend owed me a favor, so I took him up on it. He is a parrot breeder and trainer. That's why Mango Bango can say Sara's name. He also has many exotic animals such as the chameleon."

That made sense, so I asked another question.

"Grandma, do you walk in the woods much on your travels?" I asked.

"No, not much at all; I walked through the redwood forest, though. That was quite a sight. There were trees with enough volume for me and your grandpa to live in comfortably." Grandma pulled her PB&J from my backpack and took a bite.

"Why does Grandpa spend all his time in front of the TV?" I asked.

"He is tired, and he used to be an alcoholic," Grandma replied. Hearing her say that made me think of the diary I had found in the car.

"Where did you and Mom live when she was growing

up?"

"We moved around a lot. But don't you already know where we lived? For a year we lived right next to this place. The house burnt down, I think, a few years after we moved out. It was right where that trailer is now."

I gasped, right next to our house?! That must be why Mom got this place!

"What did you and Grandpa do for jobs, if you moved so much?" I asked.

"I was a nurse, but your grandfather quit his job when your mother was young."

I couldn't believe it! Maybe the diary was Mom's when she was a little girl! But Mom didn't have a sister named Mary.

"Grandma, did you have a car that was black when Mom was young; a Ford car?" I asked.

"Yes, we did till grandpa got rid of it! Man, I was so mad at him. I asked him to take it to the metal scrapyard after taking our stuff out, but he just drove it into the woods and left it there! He didn't even get the spare change out! I would have gone and gotten it, but I didn't know about it till we were almost to our new house in California. I am still upset about that. Maybe it is still in these woods! Do you want to search for it?" Grandma asked, turning away from me.

"Not really," I said, because I already knew where it was.

"Why not? It would be a great scavenger hunt! And there should be some money in it. I would let you keep it," Grandma said, excitedly. I pondered over how to change the subject. Then I thought how.

"Did my mom have a sister? Mary?" I asked. Grandma whipped around. She looked frustrated and sad at the same time.

"What! Who told you… why… what made you think your mom had a sister named Mary. She didn't! She never did! Ever! Got that! Never! Ever!" Grandma cried out. I saw a tear leak from her right eye.

"Got that?!" Grandma yelled again.

"Yes, Grandma, I am sorry I upset you," I said. She had given me all the answers I needed. Now I knew that it was Mom's diary, and she had a sister. What happened to her? Did she die? That was what I needed to find out. But why had Mom never mentioned her?

"Grandma, can we go home?" I asked, anxious to tell

Erica this news.

"Oh, dear, I am so sorry. I didn't mean to yell at you! Just there was no one named…Mary," Grandma had trouble saying that name.

"It isn't you. I am just getting eaten by bugs," I lied.

"Ok, if you really want to go, I will take you home," Grandma sighed. I could tell she didn't really want to leave, and I felt bad. But I probably couldn't take it back now.

We traveled through the woods to the creek and walked over on a dead tree that looked sort of fresh. It was wet so we had to be careful not to slip.

Once we were back in the yard, I thanked Grandma and sprinted toward the house. Almost there! I ran inside flung open my backpack and drew out my sandwich. Once it was on the counter, I ran to find Mom.

"Mom! Mo-o-o-om! Mom!" I shouted, searching for her.

"I am in my bedroom!" Mom called back. I ran into her room and asked her where her phone was. But then I noticed something different about her. She was wearing a loose dress (that looked peculiar on her since she was pregnant), loop earrings, and eyeliner.

"It is on my desk," she replied dabbing at her makeup.

"Mom? Are you going out?" I asked.

"Yes, I am going out with your father. He has been working a lot recently, and he is getting some time off soon, so we are going out to celebrate! He gets a week off around his birthday! And of course my birthday since we have the same birthday," Mom said, pulling her dress down.

"Awesome! I hope you have fun."

"That isn't all, Morgan. We will let you take a week off from school, too. I will call the office to tell them you are staying home, sick. You haven't taken off any sick days yet, so I don't see any harm."

I couldn't believe it! Mom was letting me pretend I was sick! To hang out with Dad! *I am so excited!*

"Really? Thanks!" I replied, hopping up and down. Don't get me wrong, I like school and learning, but I hadn't seen much of my dad recently.

***

Dad picked up Mom in the driveway and drove off to the Saloff's Wine & Dine Restaurant. I went to the TV room and sat down next to Grandpa. He was watching an episode of "Wheel of Fortune".

"Did you or did you not have a daughter named Mary?" He slowly turned his head to reveal a reddened face and flaring nostrils.

"What was that? You know about Mary! Huh? She is gone! Don't speak her name again! Don't dig around in this! You hear me? Don't!" After Grandpa and I had our chat, I left to call Erica to fill her in. She seemed intrigued.

Once I told her all about my conversation with Grandpa, I thought of something else.

"And I still haven't been to your parents' petting zoo!"

"I know. We have to do that sometime! Ok, see you Saturday!"

Chapter 15: The Crazy Week Off

NEEDLESS TO SAY, Grandpa hadn't taken the Mary stunt very well. It had been a while since I asked Grandpa about Mary, and I hadn't brought it up to anyone else either. Now it was Thursday, my first day off to spend with Dad.

Erica can't wait to read more of the diary. I promised her I wouldn't read anymore without her. I almost broke that promise, yesterday, when I was really bored, but I didn't.

I am really excited today. My dad starts his week off today. I have been planning for my parents' birthdays. Grandma took me to the store to buy them presents. I used all my savings to buy them each a card and their surprise, birthday presents. It took me a while to decide what to get them, but I finally figured it out.

"Morgan! Come get your breakfast!" yelled Mom, from the kitchen.

"Sara! Ken you, too!" Grandma shouted.

I ran down the hallway in my T-shirt and jeans. I was so glad I didn't have to be at school today. Today was a field trip to the historical art museum. Not that I didn't like art and history, but I have already been there, and it wasn't very impressive. *Especially around giggling girls and boys making fart noises whenever the teacher was out of earshot. No thanks!*

I sat down. Mom set a bowl of cereal with a spoon sticking out of it in front of me. I scouted out the milk. It was still on the counter. I got up and gripped it, pouring more than my share into the bowl.

The twins didn't show up till I had already finished mine. Ken had his chameleon on his shoulder. At the moment, it was red just like his shirt.

"Where is Dad?" I asked, looking around.

"He is still sleeping. Work is stressful, you know?"

"Yeah, I know," but that was when I heard his voice.

"Where are my 'chillens'?" asked Dad, coming into the room. 'Chillens' was what he called the twins and me when we were younger.

"DAD!!!" I raced to him. He had been working so hard, I barely saw him.

"Hey, Sweet Pie!" Dad replied, hugging me.

"Today is your day, so what are we doing first?" Dad asked.

"Let's go take a walk in the woods!" I said. "Or we could swim! I haven't swum in a while, and swimming season is almost over."

"Sure! Just let me eat some breakfast first." As soon as Dad finished his breakfast, we decided to get our swimming suits on.

We were all ready to get into the pool, after neglecting it for so long. The only attention it had gotten, recently, was Mom adding chlorine to keep it germ free and checking the pH to keep it balanced. I was glad for a warm enough day to get at least one more swim in!

"Cannonball!" the twins cried, in unison.

"Good one, guys!" Mom yelled. She stuck her toes over the edge and kicked the refreshing water.

"Make way!" my dad yelled, standing on one side of the

deck.

"I am coming in…Cannonball!" he yelled, rolling himself into a tiny ball. He plunged under the surface of the water, making a tsunami for the rest of us.

"Dad! You made it a wave pool," I cried, laughing.

After the pool fun, we had a quick shower. We decided to play Crazy Eights. The twins weren't really into it, so they went on their new I-pods to play Angry Birds.

"Only twenty minutes on that I-pod! It hurts your eyes!" Mom called to the twins, who had taken to the couch in the other room.

"OK!" they yelled back. After playing Crazy Eights and Uno for roughly twenty minutes, Mom went to tell the twins to put away their I-pods. But when she saw them, she immediately realized something was wrong.

The twins had taped their right eyes closed. "Sara! Ken! Why is one of your eyes taped shut?" Mom cried, exasperated.

"You said we could only play on the I-pod for twenty minutes because it hurt our eyes," said Sara.

"So we decided, if we only used one eye at a time, we

could play twice as long, twenty for the left eye and twenty for the right!" Ken explained.

"Ha, ha, very funny, that isn't going to work," Mom said, scowling.

"Now how are we going to get that tape off without pulling your eyelashes out?" asked Mom. The twins pulled. Nothing happened. They didn't scream, and no hairs got pulled out.

Still, I just couldn't help myself. "Oh, no! You pulled out your eyelashes! Ah-h-h-h-h!" I screamed, pointing at their faces. The twins cried in return, putting both of their hands on their faces feeling for hair. Then they charged off to the bathroom to see for themselves.

"Morgan! That was very irresponsible and rude," Mom said, frowning at me.

"Sorry Mom, I couldn't help it!" I said, trying to keep from laughing. Then I heard a little chuckle coming from behind me. Grandma and Dad had heard the whole thing. They, too, couldn't resist the temptation of laughter.

"You lied!" the twins yelled, re-entering the room. Sara still had red blotches under her eyes from crying.

"Can we play another twenty minutes with the other eye?" Ken asked, hiccupping.

"No, you should have asked before you did that! You might have hurt your eye; it was working twice as hard without the other one," said Mom.

"Fine!" The twins raced outside, probably to go to the treehouse. I was sure they were mad at me.

"So what do you want to do now?" Dad asked, sitting down.

"Oh! Let's play Euchre!" Grandma said, going over to shuffle the cards at the table.

"How do you play that again?" I asked. So for the next ten minutes Grandma, Dad, and Mom taught me the rules of four-person Euchre; it turned out to be my favorite card game ever. Too bad it required four players; otherwise I could teach it to Erica, so we could play it after school sometimes. The two-person version wasn't as fun, however, I thought.

After that, Dad wanted to hang out with the twins, too. We went looking for them. They were in the pirate ship.

"AR-R-R, ye, Scurvy Dogs! Hoist the anchor, and let us set sail!" Dad yelled, pulling himself up to the ship's main deck.

“AR-R-R!” we all replied.

“Ken! I assign you as my first mate. Sara you can be our super-important lookout. Morgan! You are my weapons master!” Dad yelled, revealing gifts for all of us out of his pockets for the game. He must have grabbed them just before we left the house.

“Morgan! You get this sharp knife!” Dad said, throwing me a fake knife with a covering over the fake blade.

“Sara! You are the lookout so I am presenting you with a telescope,” Dad handed her a pretend telescope that you could barely see through.

“Ken! As my first mate, you get a compass! All of you will be paid five gold doubloons per day for your hardships as my crew from my personal stash in the hold.” Dad must have been talking about the chest full of fake gold in the belly of the ship.

“I am coming to steal your treasure!” Mom yelled, arriving on the deck.

“A thief! Weapons master! You know what to do!”

“Right, Captain, on it!” I pulled my knife and slowly

stalked towards Mom. She was holding two fencing swords and two suits in her arms.

"Let's fight! Throw on your armor!" I couldn't believe Mom had gotten us fencing gear.

I quickly put on my gear and helmet holding out my sword. Mom finished putting on her gear and Dad said on guard!

"Where did you get this gear?" I asked her.

"The suits were in with Grandma's clothes," Mom said, shrugging. "I just bought some fencing swords to go with it." I nodded. That made sense. It seemed peculiar that she had one in my size though. Oh, well, it sure appeared that Grandma liked to collect clothes.

I made the first move, poking Mom in the chest with the rubber-tipped sword.

"1 to zip!" Dad exclaimed. I was surprised that I had already made a strike!

"First to get to five is the winner," I could tell Mom was getting worked up. She didn't like to lose.

Mom struck! I put up my sword and blocked her.

"Hah!" I cried. I swung at her again, but she stopped me. She started stepping towards me. I backed up to the side of the ship.

"Go, Morgan!" the twins chanted.

"What about me?" Mom asked, looking over at them. I took my chance and poked Mom in the stomach.

"You are the bad guy, Mom," replied Ken. I stuck her twice more, almost winning, but Mom got me a second time. Finally I won 5 to 3.

"Woo-hoo, Morgan!" cried the twins, clapping.

"I slayed the thief, now throw her overboard!" I bellowed, bowing to all.

"I will get you next time!" Mom said, taking off her fencing outfit. I took mine off, too.

I didn't play the pirate game much longer. It got kind of boring so I went back inside. Mom was in my room holding a book of some kind.

"What are you looking at, Mom?" I asked. I came closer to her, and then I saw what it was. She was reading the diary from the woods, her diary, the diary that had been lost for years.

“Where did you get this?” she asked, tears in her eyes.

“Mom I…,”

“Where did you get this?” Mom asked, calmly, trying not to burst into tears.

“I found it in the woods,” I said, plainly. I didn’t want to mention the automobile.

“Where in the woods? Was it in something?” Mom asked.

“It was in, uh, a bag, a shopping bag,” I lied.

“Have you read it?”

“Not much, just a few pages. Who is Mary?” I asked. I knew it must have been a sensitive subject, and it probably wasn’t the best time to ask it, but I did.

“I don’t know who wrote the diary, so how would I know who Mary is?” she replied. But I knew she was lying. Why would she be crying otherwise? She left the room with the book, but I didn’t object. Erica would be upset, but not anymore than Mom.

Chapter 16: Steal It Back!

I SIMPLY SAT IN MY ROOM for a little while pondering what had just happened. I wasn't sure what to think of it. I wasn't even totally positive it was Mom's diary. But there was one thing for sure. Mom, Grandma and Grandpa knew Mary (the sister of the girl from the diary).

I was eager to read that diary. I felt like if I read it, I would uncover some juicy secret. It was like reading half of the best book ever and then not getting to read the ending. I wanted to read it to find out what happened to the characters and which way the plot would turn. I got up and looked around. I wanted to find something to do. Something, anything, to keep me from seeing Mom and getting plunged head first into an uncomfortable disagreement or silence.

I went to Sara's room and checked on her bird. It looked like it needed more water, so I took the liberty of changing its water out.

After I played with it a bit, I put it back and went to see Dad. He and the twins were turning on the TV.

Grandpa was sitting in the corner looking pretty angry so I presumed they had cut in on his show.

"Hey what are you guys going to watch?" I asked sitting down next to Ken.

"I don't know yet. We are deciding between 'The Croods' and 'Wreck-It Ralph,'" Dad replied, holding up two DVD's.

"Oh that is easy. If you can't figure it out, do a coin toss," I said, running to my room to grab a penny.

When I returned, Dad called heads, 'The Croods'. I flipped the coin and jumped out of the way. It landed on the coffee table.

I walked over to it and squinted, "Tails!" I cried. I picked up the penny and made it disappear into my pocket.

I offered to put the movie in for Dad and took it out of the case. When we finally got past all the warnings and copyrights we hit play. It was a great movie. My favorite character was the girl with a raspy voice and the candy in her hair. She reminded me of the twins in a way, mischievous, smart, funny, and she was a smart- aleck.

***

The next day, aka Mom and Dad's birthdays, started out great. They read my cards. Mom read hers first:

Dear Mom,
Happy 35th birthday! You are the best mom ever. Thank you for all the awesome things you do for me!

I have some great stuff planned for today. I hope you like your presents.
Your daughter,
Morgan

Dad's letter was a touch different:

Dear Dad,
Happy Birthday! You are now three and a half times my age! I am so glad you were able to take time off to spend your birthday with us. I love you!
Your daughter,
Morgan

Next, they opened up the presents. I got Mom a shirt that said: BEST MOM EVER! I also made her a bracelet. I got Dad a shirt, too. It said the same thing, only instead of Mom, it said Dad. I also gave him a hat that I had embroidered words into. The little stitching said: To Dad from Morgan. The twins also got them gifts. They had drawn pictures for them.

After that we went to the restaurant. I had called ahead and told them to sing 'Happy Birthday' when we walked in. As soon as we came through the doors, the staff broke out in song.

Mom and Dad jumped back in surprise, but quickly recovered. It was cool that everyone eating in the restaurant pitched in to sing with us. Soon it was time to go home for cake and a surprise.

Mom and Dad were treated like royalty. They both got a piece of cake with candles on top. Then we showed them their BIG birthday surprise. I had been secretly rehearsing a play with the twins. We acted out the short story that I had written during the summer.

The twins got a little restless when it came to the part where they were stuck in a coma, but they were, otherwise, superb! Everyone cheered and clapped and called for an encore afterwards.

After that was over we watched another movie. Then we had a short swim. Now that all the fun stuff was over, I was excited to see Erica. I hadn't seen her for a while!

***

"Erica!" I cried, running to the car that was sitting out in our driveway. We had a brief hug then I walked her to the door.

"Hey, where is Eric?" I asked, looking back at the car.

"Oh, yeah, he is still mad at the twins for being rude," Erica replied.

"Still?! Man, he can hold a grudge." We walked over to my room and Erica set down her purse.

"Alright, where is the diary?" Erica asked, excitedly.

"Mom saw it and confiscated it," I answered, sadly.

"You haven't taken it back yet? Come on let's go find it!" Erica said, turning toward the door.

"What? You want me to steal from my mom's room?" I asked, stepping back.

"It sounds bad when you say it like that, but just think.

She took it from you first. If you just took something that was yours out of her room it wouldn't be stealing!" I thought about what she had said. It was true, but Mom had purposely taken it from me! That means it would be stealing if I took it back.

I explained my theory to Erica, but she only shook her head. "You think about these things too hard. Just do, don't think. By the time your mom comes back to her room, she will have forgotten all about the diary. That is how older adults are," explained Erica, matter-of-factly.

I knew it was still a bad idea, and that Mom wouldn't just forget about the diary that had made her cry. I was unsure, but I decided to go along with Erica; I really wanted to finish reading it.

"Alright fine, let's do it," I agreed, following her to the door. We had tiptoed down the hallway, looking around to make sure we weren't caught.

"Shh!" I said. Erica had stepped on a loose floorboard making it creak.

"Sorry!" Erica whispered. I slowly turned the handle on Mom's door, and we creeped inside. I wasn't really sure where it was, so I told Erica to keep watch while I searched.

She stepped out the door and closed it behind her. I looked everywhere! I looked under the bed, in the closet, in the drawers, in the bathroom, behind the TV, in the bed, and under the dresser.

Then I heard Erica from outside. "Hello, Mrs. Sill! How are you?" I froze. Thinking where I should hide, I stepped into the closet. From inside I couldn't hear Erica anymore.

Then the door opened and my heart started to beat tenfold. I squinted shut my eyes. Then the knob to the closet started to turn.

In burst Erica, "Morgan, your mom said we couldn't play war in her room." Erica said, winking at me.

I was relieved! Erica had come up with a good excuse! After we hightailed out of Mom's room, Erica asked me if I had gotten it. I slipped the tiny booklet out of my shirt and showed it to Erica. She smiled and took it out of my hands, flipping enthusiastically through the pages.

We ended up reading the whole diary in a little over an hour. It was cool to learn more about Mom. On the other hand, we found out about the ugly truth of Mom's younger sister, Mary.

It was so sad I almost couldn't read through the last

page. It went like this:

Dear Stupid Diary,
I can barely write this last page of my diary. I flip to the beginning and think about how happy things were before Mary died from cancer.

I should have let her go to the thrift store with me and Jean's birthday. She would have loved the triple chocolate ice-cream sundaes.

I still can't comprehend what it was like going through the treatments and I was there!

Mom is only making things worse. She is throwing away every picture of Mary and her toys. We are moving to California. It is like she is trying to forget Mary all together. This is the last time I write in this diary, so, bye.
-Victoria

I cried while reading it, and so did Erica. The diary had taken us through all of the hardships that Mary and her sister (my mom) had gone through.

I almost wished we hadn't found the diary in the first place. Now I understood; no wonder it was such a sensitive subject to all my family members.

Chapter 17: The White Christmas

"MORGAN!!! MORGAN!!!" the twins cried, shaking me awake from a great dream. I was glad they had though. It was Christmas morning, over three months after Erica and I had learned about Mary.

Mom was going to have her baby any day, and we couldn't hold our excitement in much longer. I wished we could have visited our cousins, but Mom wasn't fit for travel.

I looked at the clock. It was 4:49 A. M. The twins always got up early on Christmas morning. I raced down the hallway with them to the tree. Around it was a stack of gifts; they were all piled on top of each other. The lights on the tree reflected off the Christmas ornaments hanging from the branches. Lots of the ornaments were homemade from previous Christmases. The lights blinked on and off green, red, blue, and yellow.

Mom and Dad had fallen asleep by the tree, that way they would wake up when we did. They were on a blow-up mattress. We quickly jump-started them awake and resorted to present opening. It was like my birthday all over again.

"Daddy did you see Santa last night?" asked Sara.

"No, we didn't. He must have snuck right past us while we were sleeping," Dad replied.

We played with the new Wii video games for an hour, and then with Ken and Sara's new Legos. Grandma and Grandpa watched as we skipped from one thing to the next.

We even got Grandma to dance with the Wii. Mom wanted to try it, but she wasn't feeling great with the baby coming so soon.

When we took a break we went to the kitchen to make some cookies and eggnog. It was only just getting daylight, but Mom and Dad were ok with it. The sugar cookies tasted so good after being plunged into a glass of nog. Mom made the best!

When it was finally daylight, we sprinted outside and into the freshly fallen snow. Last Christmas, we only had a smidgen of snow, but this year it was over a foot high.

It seemed like we were out playing forever. We had a snowball fight. The twins were awful at making the snowballs round. It was even hard for me. The snow wouldn't stick together! I wished we could stack them like in the movies, but in reality, it didn't work out. I guessed the snow was not wet enough.

We ran to the creek and scooted over the ice with our boots. Mom scolded Dad when she came out to find Ken had fallen through the ice and gotten soaked from the knees down.

"Well what about you?" Dad exclaimed. "You are over eight months pregnant. You should go inside!"

Ken just about froze, even his nose looked blue. Mom hurried him inside and stripped him out of his sopped clothing. Then she wrapped him in about twenty blankets. I am exaggerating a bit, but it seemed that way.

"Mom! He is more wrapped up than a mummy!" As soon as I said that, Sara dashed out of the room. I was hoping that she wasn't planning something. But she had been; she came down the hallway wrapped in toilet paper.

"I am a mummy!" Sara exclaimed, the paper falling down to her calves and trailing on the floor.

"Sara! Do you know how much toilet paper costs? Just because we have more money now, doesn't mean we can just waste it!" Mom sighed, exasperated with Sara's wastefulness.

"O-o-o-o-o-o-o-o-o-o-o-o-o-o-o-o-o! I am a mummy!" Sara said, tripping over the paper trails.

As Sara stood back up, I corrected her. "You sound like a ghost. Mummy's don't make that noise,"

"Uh-uh! I am a mummy, and I just made that sound so mummy's say it, too!" Sara snapped.

"Whatever!" I replied, rolling my eyes. Then my thoughts changed to the new baby. I was exited yet a little nervous. It was like starting at a new school. When I started at Raccoon Elementary School, I wasn't sure what to expect!

How are things going to change? What will it be like? Will I like it? Will she like me?

Then other thoughts crossed my mind: things that I couldn't relate to my new school: like would Mom still have time for me after the baby arrived?

I wondered if her having four kids would take away the

time we would have together. Like when we went out to eat, just us, or went shopping for clothes.

Good thing Grandma and Grandpa, well at least Grandma, is here to help out. Grandma seemed, however, like the type to hover over a baby like a fly hovers over pie.

I looked around for Grandma. I hadn't seen her since this morning. Now it was noon, and I was hungry.

"Mom, are we going to eat soon?" I asked, grasping my stomach and dramatically moaning.

"Yes, we will soon, drama queen!" she replied, laughing. At least it took the spotlight off Sara. Mom was really starting to get irritated with her.

Ken was still shivering, so Mom returned to caring for him. She forced him to drink her healing sniffles tea, and then she added another blanket to the Ken bundle. Once Ken had warmed up, he asked if he could go back outside.

"Sorry Ken. You only have one snowsuit and it is soaking wet. You are going to have to play inside now." Ken burst into tears. I felt so bad for him! He loved the snow so much and besides it was Christmas.

"Bye Ken! I am going to play war with Morgan in the

snow!" Sara said, pulling some of the toilet paper out of her hair.

"But that isn't fair to Ken! You guys play in here for now," Mom said. My shoulders slumped. I felt bad for Ken, but not bad enough to stay inside on a snowy Christmas. I might not have another chance!

"Mom! That is not fair! I never get to play in the snow!" I pouted, crossing my arms. I felt like I would cry, but of course I didn't. If I did, I would be more of a baby than my soon-to-be sister.

"Morgan! Don't talk back! What would you do if you were the one that got soaked?"

"I would let Sara and Ken go on out and play while I watched a Christmas movie."

"It is still no. But that movie idea is a good one. That is something we can all do!" Mom said, kissing Ken on the head and racing to the remote control.

Moms flipped through the various channels till she came across a kid-friendly Christmas movie. It was one of those cartoon ones that weren't very good.

"Rudolf the red-nose reindeer, had a very shiny nose," the twins sang along. So I went to my room to read. I happened to have a Christmas book on the shelf. But I couldn't concentrate enough to read. I was thinking about the baby. I still had some concerns. Would I have to change the stinky diapers when Mom and Dad were busy?

I went into the new baby's room. The twins and I had been forbidden to enter it, but I really wanted to see it. I had asked earlier why I wasn't allowed to go in. It was because our parents didn't want the twins to mess it up; if I was allowed to go in, but they weren't… well you get the picture.

The room was so cute. The walls were painted a calm green. There was a crib in one corner and a chest full of little teddy bears. There was a little set of drawers full of baby clothes, and there was a small bookshelf full of childish books.

The closet held baby food, bibs, bottles, and a pack of pacifiers, a couple small blankets, educational toys, and a few other things.

They had a mobile hanging over the crib. I turned it on and it started to spin and produced a soft music.

Seeing all of her things in the room made me appreciate how real this whole baby thing was. *I am going to have another sister!*

Poor Ken! He will have a bunch of sisters and no brothers! I browsed around for a moment longer then snuck back out, closing the door so that no one would know I had gone in there.

When I went into the TV room, I saw that the twins were still engrossed in the show. I went to the kitchen to sneak another cookie.

Dad had beaten me to it, however. He was stuffing his face with a snowman sugar cookie. "Dad!" I cried, laughing.

"What? I am guessing you were coming here to do the same thing!" He said, making me smile guiltily.

While the twins were occupied with the show, we ate cookies till we were stuffed. "What do you think about the new baby coming along? Are you happy about it or not?"

"I am excited, but I have pros and cons," I said and left it at that.

"Do you want to see what we did to the baby's room while Mom and the twins are occupied?" asked Dad, putting away the cookie tray that was now half empty. I just about choked on my milk. I was surprised that Dad offered to let me see it, but I accepted his invitation even though I had already been into the room, secretly.

"What did you think?" asked Dad, as we left.

"I have one question, why do you have baby food when the baby won't be able to eat it for many months?"

"Oh yeah, your Mom wanted to be prepared, and they last a while," he replied. I nodded, but I still thought it was odd.

Finally, when the movie was over, the twins and I went downstairs to the under-the-stairs hideout. We call it "The Fort". We liked to draw on the fort's walls.

It already had a fair amount of drawing from the twins, but we could always find room. Especially me, since I could reach higher.

I felt like Michelangelo, the famous artist, drawing on the ceiling of the Sistine Chapel. I also wrote on the walls things like this: **Morgan was here! Morgan Rocks! This is Morgan's Fort. Morgan is the new Michelangelo!**

***

The twins wept when it was time to go to bed. "But it is

Christmas! Please let us stay up." They sobbed, tears streaming down their red cheeks.

"No, Christmas ended at 8:30," Mom fibbed, but the twins still wanted to stay up.

Finally, Mom and Dad separated them and put them in their bedrooms. It was lights out. I went to bed shortly after. I was zonked!

Chapter 18: It Is Finally Time!

DECEMBER 28, three days after Christmas, we were all sitting around the table having breakfast. I was eating a waffle when all of a sudden Mom groaned and bent over.

"What is wrong?" The twins asked, with a hint of worry in their voices.

"I think I am having the baby!" Mom bellowed, grabbing her stomach.

"Everyone get in the car!" Dad yelled, quickly turning off the waffle maker. We didn't even turn out the lights as we left.

I managed to grab a book on the way out, but that was it. The twins complained that they didn't get their toys or, at least, their I-pods.

Dad shushed them and opened the passenger door for

Mom. She slowly climbed in, trying not to moan too loudly.

"Take deep breaths!" Dad reminded her, slamming the car door. He forgot to buckle in the twins, so I did. Dad quickly left the driveway and was racing full speed down our road towards the hospital. I crossed my fingers that we wouldn't get pulled over for speeding, by the police. It only took us five minutes to reach the hospital at this speed.

Mom was put in a wheelchair as soon as we arrived and was rolled down the hallway. "Is Mommy hurt?" Sara asked, wide-eyed.

"No Honey, she is just getting ready to deliver you a new sister," said Dad, holding Sara's hand tight. Dad hurried into the room where they had put Mom, but we had to stay in the waiting room. He made us promise not to move, and told me to keep a sharp eye on the twins.

I sat between the twins so I could watch them better. "What will our new sister be like?" Ken asked.

I tried to think up a good answer, but really I was clueless. "I have no idea," I said, ruffing up his hair.

"I wish it was a boy," said Ken, his head drooping.

"That isn't going to happen," I told him. We waited a long time. What was taking so long?

I now regretted that I had taken my book along. I was too energized to read it anyway. It was just a burden to carry around. I started to drum on it with my hands, but a nurse came over. She told me I was being annoying, and she couldn't concentrate on her paperwork, so I stopped.

Annoyed myself, I set the book on the floor and started drumming on my legs. She rolled her eyes and shot me an unkind look. I decided I had better not get her too upset, so I stopped.

After what seemed like an agonizing 10 hours, Dad finally came out of the room. He was wearing a weird surgeon's mask and was holding three others out to us.

"Put these on," he said, handing one to each of us. "It keeps us from giving her germs," he explained.

I nodded then put mine on. Dad had to help the twins put on their masks. "Are you ready to meet your new sister?" asked Dad, opening the door.

"Yes," we replied. We followed Dad into the tiny hospital room. Mom was cradling a bundle in her arms.

I hung over Mom and stared down into the eyes of a little girl the size of a loaf of bread. I couldn't help saying… "Aww," as the wrinkly thing gripped my finger and stuck out her tongue.

"What is her name?" I asked, looking up at Mom. She thought for a moment before saying the most beautiful name ever.

"Karenna Lee Sill,"

Coming Soon

The Morgan Series

Morgan's Baby Sister

Book 3

Book three is filled with triple the trouble,
so don't miss out!

Golden Keeper

A great fantasy book for teens!

Olympian Bound

This novel for teens
really tugs at your heart strings!

Interview with the Author, KD

Q: When did you realize you wanted to be an author?

A: I always loved to write even before I knew I wanted to be an author. When I was younger, I wanted to be a singer, then a surgeon or a chiropractor. But when I was ten I finally decided I what I wanted to be, an author.

Q: Is the Morgan Series based on you?

A: There are a few of my experiences in my books but the vast majority is made up.

Q: What is the first book you ever wrote?

A: The first book I ever wrote was called "Bad Lilly." It was only a short story and I was four but at the time I was very proud. It hasn't been published yet but someday I may turn it into a children's book.

Q: What inspired you to write your first novel?

A: I had many inspirations including my brother Darik and our cousin Guy, but mainly it was my love of reading and writing.

Q: How long does it take you to write your novels?

A: My first novel, "Morgan's Summer," took two years since I was working on many others. "Morgan's New School" took one year, my first poem book took 6 days and my novel, "Golden Keeper" took four and a half months.

Q: What did you do to celebrate finishing your novels?

A: We didn't do anything to celebrate my first novel but my second one we went to a restaurant called Milers Ale House and bowling.

Q: How old were you when you finished "Morgan's Summer" and "Morgan's New School."

A: I was ten years old when I finished "Morgan's Summer" and eleven when I finished "Morgan's New School."

Q: What is your favorite thing to do, other than writing?

A: I enjoy golfing, wakeboarding, playing my guitar, pottery, reading, rock climbing, swimming and many other activities.

Q: What is your favorite game?

A: My favorite game is the one I made up myself. It is a game that goes with my Morgan Series Books. That way, my readers can have fun with pretending to be as mischievous as the twins. We are in the process of making it available to the public at www.kdlwrites.com.

Visit www.kdlwrites.com to learn about KD,
her novels, and more!

About the Book:

Morgan's daily drama continues in this sequel to Morgan's sequel. Not only does Morgan have to deal with her brother and sister's devious schemes, but she also has to put up with her terrible teacher. At least she meets a new friend to help her through tough times. Exploration of her new stomping grounds reveals a family secret. To top it all off, she finally gets to meet her new baby sister. Let the adventures of her new school begin!

About KD (The Author)

KD was born in 2003. She lives in the country near Bloomington, IN. She has two dogs and a snake. KD is homeschooled by her grandmother, DD, who is a retired school teacher. She has a younger brother, Darik. She enjoys swimming, playing her guitar, wakeboarding, gold, and other activities. However, writing is her true passion. She wrote her first book, "Bad Lily" when she was four. Her first article was published in a youth magazine when she was eight. Shortly afterwards, she started this series, finishing the first book, Morgan's Summer, before her eleventh birthday. This is the second book in the series, and she is currently working on many other novels.

47633122R00116

Made in the USA
Charleston, SC
14 October 2015